Purse Pet
A Shrink Inc Novel

copyright 2017 Taedis

Purse Pet

0: Doll Commando

Wearing doll clothes isn't as fun as it sounds.

Remember when you were three and the tag in your t-shirt felt like the worst thing ever? Now imagine wearing a dress made of that feeling and you have some idea what wearing doll clothes is like. If you try not to think about it too hard you might be able to trick yourself into thinking that you're wearing a normal dress, but it won't be long before you shift your shoulder a little or turn at the waist just a bit. Then you'll feel it. Feel how the fabric doesn't quite hang the way it should. How rough it is against your little skin. How it feels like your wearing a costume instead of an outfit.

As bad as the dress is the underwear is worse. Don't even get me started on wearing a doll bra. I suppose they give great support for molded plastic boobs, but mine are all natural and not digging the dolly bra.

Oddly enough I was fine with the plastic shoes.

I was carried into a room full of women I knew. A room full of witnesses and judges who were about to decide where I belonged. And to who. Or is that whom? I can never remember. Anyway, the women were seated around this huge mahogany round table that would have made King Arthur jealous.

I … wasn't.

My tiny butt was plopped down on the bottom of the wheel in my luxurious hamster cage. My elbows rested on my knees, my chin rested on my small fists. And yes, I was wearing doll clothes. And no, it wasn't the worst thing I had to wear since getting shrunk.

I felt like the pot in the world's weirdest poker tournament.

The cage was to remind me what I was now – a pet. A pet who belonged to one of the women sitting in the real chairs wearing real clothes taking time out from their real lives to decide my future. When this was all over and the comfy chairs were pushed under the mahogany one of these women would stuff me in her purse and take me to my forever home.

My cousin Carly was in one of those seats, but she wasn't going to be my owner. She loved me more than I deserved, but tiny people are out of her price range. No one bothered telling me why she was here. I just assumed it was to give testimony about the fight in the woods. And the explosion. They wouldn't let us see each other until now. I'll give the Stovent scientists credit; they did as good a job fixing her burns as they did me.

Carly smiled at me. After all the stupid things I'd done she still loved me. Carly, why didn't I listen to you in the first place?

They must have dunked Jordan in the same bacta tank as Carly and me. She looked perfect. Physically. But there was something just behind her eyes that told me she was being haunted by my mistakes. Technically, she was the woman who bought me, but her legal status was almost as messed up as mine. Heck, for a couple weeks I kinda sorta owned her.

Jordan was huddled close to Maria. The maid turned millionaire kept a reassuring hand on Jordan's arm. Maria probably had the strongest claim to me – a six figure receipt. She'd been giving me the stink eye ever since the intern plopped my cage down in the middle of the table.

I didn't blame her.

The intern was Lauren. I want to go on record as saying that Lauren is a dick. Also, she was my trainer after I'd been shrunk. She made me run through literal hoops in-between doing humiliating and frankly juvenile things to me. Of all the women seated at that table she was the only one I hated. The only good thing about her being here was the nothing chance that I'd be leaving with her.

Lauren sat at the left hand of Claire. Claire was the middle manager who got me to sign on the shrunken line. The contract that turned me from up and coming literary genius Rebecca Hogarth into Becky the pet. I didn't like or hate Claire, I was just surprised that they didn't have somebody higher up the food chain handling this for Stovent. At least she and Lauren weren't in on the Becky lottery.

I hoped.

That left McCaskill.

There wasn't a literal "head of the table." That's the whole point of a round table. But if any of these women were sitting at the figurative head it would be McCaskill. Even though she was more of a Morgan Le Fey than King Arthur.

McCaskill was Tina's lawyer. Tina was twenty year old singing sensation Tina Jordan. Even if you don't know her name you've heard at least one of her songs. Or you just hate music. I loved Tina more than anything else in this world. At least at the beginning. Loved her so much that I was willing to to be shrunk knee high to a Barbie doll cause that's what she wanted. Some musicians don't want brown M&Ms; Tina wanted a little woman she could love and carry around in her purse like a bichon frise. She was supposed to adopt me, but my life sidestepped into farce and that didn't happen.

Tina couldn't make it to this hearing cause she was in the middle of her ArgenTINA! World Tour and couldn't fit me into her schedule. I was devastated when I found out she wasn't gonna show. I guess that's just the sort of thing I'm gonna have to get used to if I end up Tina's pet. It's not like you fly halfway across the globe every time your dog had the sniffles.

McCaskill was there to make sure that Tina Jordan got what she wanted. I just didn't know if she still wanted me.

"What's that doing here?" McCaskill didn't need to say my name or look at me for everyone to know she was talking about me.

I tried not to look at McCaskill. She wasn't my type. She was middle aged, super corporate, and a control freak. The kind of woman who probably spent her teen years touching herself while Maggie Thatcher droned on the radio. All those years in the conservative closet had made her kinkier than Lauren. The only difference was I kinda wanted McCaskill to do those things to me. There was something about the old control freak that pushed buttons in my head that turned my knees into rubber and left stains in my little dolly drawers.

"It's time we heard Becky's version of events." Claire said.

"Why?"

"It's a complicated case, Ms. McCaskill. I'm hoping Becky can shed some light on a few things that aren't that clear right now."

"Translation – my company screwed up and I'm looking for any excuse to get us out of a massive federal lawsuit."

McCaskill's dominant tone, even directed at Claire, was pushing those buttons I was talking about. I pulled my thighs together and tried to think of anything but submitting to this powerful woman.

"It's a bit more complicated than that."

"It always is." McCaskill concluded.

"I don't see the point of this either." Maria said. "We already know what happened. If we give her the chance to talk she's just going to try to lie her way out of it. I've spent more time with her than anyone else at this table … who isn't related to her. She's just going to tell us whatever she needs to to get out of trouble."

"That hurts, Maria." I stood up from the bottom of my hamster wheel and walked over to the bars of my cage. I put my hands up high on the bars and pulled myself up as high as my tiny arms let me. The extra inch or two didn't lend me the gravitas I'd hoped. "I know things went pear shaped between us. That was mostly my fault. But after everything, I was hoping we could get beyond that and …"

My Captain Kirk-like speech was cut off before I got to the good part. An intense quick blast of water slammed into my chest and pushed me back from the cage bars. It felt like being hit by a high pressure fire hose for just a second. I shook my head and tried to figure out what the eff just happened. I heard Maria start to say something, but whatever it was got drowned out by another blast. This one didn't feel as strong, but it soaked everything from the hair on the top of my head to the bottoms of my plastic doll shoes.

"Whoever's doing that please …"

The third wave pushed me back before I could finish. The plastic shoes tried to find traction on the wet cage floor, but I might as well have had roller skates strapped to my feet. I barely managed to land on my butt instead of my head. Lucky for me I was ridiculously light at this size or I'd have hurt more than my pride.

I lay there on the floor of the hamster cage in a rapidly growing puddle. I was soaked through. My red doll dress clung to me like a teenager on a second date.

"STOP DOING THAT!" I screamed as I tried to pull myself up.

"Bad Becky! No bark!" Lauren yelled back at me. "The grown ups are talking."

I looked at her just in time to see her aim a giant spray bottle at me and pull the trigger. Like she was disciplining a cat who was scratching something she wasn't supposed to even be near.

I told you Lauren was a dick, didn't I?

"Do that again, bitch and I'l shove that bottle so far up your ass you'll be able to gargle with it."

I managed to see my cousin rip the bottle out of the dick intern's hands. Carly looked as serious as she sounded.

"Thanks, Carly." I managed to sputter out.

"I understand that Becky may not be the most reliable witness." Claire went on like her toady Lauren hadn't just pre-waterboarded me. "We're prepared to inject her with a truth drug."

"That can't be legal." Carly said, returning to her seat with Lauren's spray bottle.

"Becky hasn't had human rights in months, Miss Vintner." Claire said. "The federal government doesn't even classify her as an animal.

Not for legal protections, anyway. You'll find we can do whatever we want to her."

Carly's face said it all – she knew the law; she just didn't like it.

"And how are we to know that this truth drug works?" McCaskill asked.

"Yeah." Maria said. "For all we know you could pump her full of saline and have her tell some prearranged cock and bull story."

"If either of you ladies doubt the efficacy of our patented truth drug I can arrange a demonstration. I'll just need your body weight and a notarized consent form." Claire said. Maybe she wasn't as meek and mild as I thought.

"Are you serious?" Maria asked.

"I have one hundred percent confidence in my company's technology, Ms. Alvarez."

"Can't I just say 'no' this once?"

I pulled myself to my feet. Wearing doll clothes sucked; wearing wet doll clothes would have been a new level of Hell had Dante lived long enough to write a sequel.

"I know you can do anything you want with me, but the thing is I've had some pretty bad drug experiences since I got Aliced down to size. I promise you I'll tell the truth. Heck I'll even stand on a Bible and give you my oath."

"Pets can't take oaths." McCaskill said.

I felt an erotic spark race down my spine. What was wrong with me? It was like she was Frau Blucher and I was the horse. Only in a lot of very very different ways that my brain didn't have time to navigate right now.

"I'm ok with the drug if you are." Maria said to McCaskill.

"Fine." McCaskill said.

"Lauren?" Claire turned to the intern who already had the needle out.

"Where's that going?" I had a bad feeling about this. "Exactly."

"Bend over." Lauren ordered.

"Seriously." Things were getting better and better. "Do something, Carly. You're an attorney. Sorta."

"I'm sorry, sweetie."

"Fine." I said. "Get it over with."

Lauren laid the loaded syringe down on the table and played around with the catch on my cage. It took her a couple tries to get it open. At one point she jostled the table a little. When you're three and a half inches tall a little table jostle translates into about a 3.2 on my new downsized richter scale. Between the quake, the water, and my plastic doll shoes I went down to my knees fast.

Lauren's giant hand reached down through the open top and wrapped themselves around my tiny shaking body. Even after all this time it still felt weird being picked up by someone like that. To feel their fingers wrap around you like you were some kind of toy. Knowing you pretty much were.

I was lifted up into the air and deposited on the dark wood table. Lauren's giant hands felt warm against my still soggy little body. I felt even colder than I had before she'd picked me up.

"Stand up and turn your back to Lauren." Claire ordered.

I obeyed. There was nothing else I could do.

"Bend over."

I did.

I felt Lauren reach down and pull up the back of my dress. She draped it over my back and let it sit there. The cheap cloth was still soaked so it was happy to stay in place. I felt cool air on my cold bare legs. The only warmth I felt was from the blush and that didn't reach my legs. I kept my eyes on the ground. The table top. And watched as water drip drip dripped off of me.

"Pull your underwear down." Lauren ordered. She sounded bored.

"Does she have to?" Carly asked. "Can't you just shoot her through them?"

"No." Was the only answer Lauren gave.

Claire didn't say anything to contradict her.

"I'm only doing this so I can moon you." I was trying to make a joke, but it fell flat. Story of my life.

I lowered my panties to my knees and held them there with both hands. My thighs were clamped together as tightly as they could be for heat and modesty.

I felt something huge, soft, and wet in a chemical way rub from just above my knees to my lower back. It took me a second to realize it had been an antiseptic wipe.

"Just a little prick." Lauren said placing the needle against my shivering right cheek.

"Yes you are."

It was probably not the smartest thing to say to someone about to stick a giant needle into your bum, but I've never been accused of making the smartest choices.

The needle was longer than my entire body and thicker than my thumb. It didn't have to go that far into my little butt, but I felt every bit of it slide into me.

Then Lauren hit the plunger and the drug was forced into me.

It was different than the other times. The others felt cool and calming. They knocked me out before I had a chance to freak out any more than I already had. This felt warm. I could feel its heat traveling through my body just a step ahead of my blood. I briefly felt like I had to pee. Real bad. But that went away.

I was feeling very light headed, but still awake when Lauren pressed a cotton ball to my butt and ordered me to apply pressure. I took my hands off my underwear and pressed the cotton against my injured butt. I didn't even notice how much of a dick Lauren was being.

"All right, Becky." Claire said. "I want you to stand up, face us, and tell us what happened to you. In your own words."

I obeyed. The back of my dress fell back down. At least as much as my hands and the cotton ball allowed it to. My underwear puddled at my feet, but going doll commando didn't bother me after getting the shot.

"It started when I was arrested."

One: A Doll Deal

--A Holding Cell--

"Remind me what we're looking at."

The detective walked back into the room carrying a paper cup of coffee and looked at the man with no jacket who had his sleeves rolled up. I didn't remember either of their names. I didn't even remember what he said his rank was.

"Rebecca Hogarth. Age 25. A long list of minor infractions going back to her juvie days. Mostly being where she wasn't supposed to be. A couple suspended sentences for trespass. A breaking and entering. Shop lifting. One count of arson when she was sixteen, but it looks like she hasn't been playing with matches since then."

"Why's she here now?" the detective sipped her coffee. I think she was bored.

"Ms. Hogarth started ramping things up over the past few months. Started writing letters and e-mails to Tina Jordan."

"The pop star my kid listens to?"

"Probably. I can't tell them apart." rolled up sleeves said. "The letters started getting more intense. Ms. Jordan's lawyers responded. Ms. Hogarth ended up breaking into Ms. Jordan's local residence. We're looking at stalking charges as well as the usual trespass, breaking and entering, resisting arrest. And she punched officer Wilson in the … he and his wife may not be having that second kid they've been working on."

"If that lawyer of her is more competent than she looks, little Becky here just might see parole before she hits menopause." The detective took another sip of coffee.

"We're right here." Carly said. She didn't sound happy.

Carly's the only attorney I could afford and also my second cousin. I'm her first client. She promised me she passed the bar, but I'm pretty sure she was lying about that, but that didn't matter cause I'm not going to trial.

"It looks like you're both here for a very long time, counsellor." the detective said.

"This is a huge misunderstanding, Ma'am." I said. "Just call Tina and she'll explain everything. Except for the part where I punched that cop in the balls. I'm really sorry about that, but I was feeling threatened and I couldn't find my pepper spray."

"Counsellor, you have ten minutes to pound some sense into your client."

The detective and the man with the rolled up sleeves walked out the door leaving Carly and me alone.

Carly started saying "fuck" over and over again as soon as the door shut.

"That is **so** not helping, Carly." I said. "You need to fix this."

"What were you thinking?" Carly asked after she stopped saying "fuck."

"I am not going to apologize for what I am."

"What are you?"

"I … am a woman in love … with another woman." I calmly explained.

"Nobody cares if you're gay."

"I love Tina and I have been arrested for it. If that isn't a clear example of homophobic fascism than tell me the Doublespeak word for what I'm trying to say."

"You're gay, cookie." Carly said. "That's great. The cops are cool with that. I'm cool with that. Hell, I'll call you Sappho Dykewomyn if it helps."

"It doesn't."

"Well maybe a snappy slogan would make you feel more comfortable."

"Not if you're going to say it with that tone of voice."

"How about this." Carly said. "Vagina, it's not just for breakfast anymore."

"I saw what you did there. Very cute, but that's not dealing with the problem of this institutional homophobia."

"Vagina, the pause that refreshes."

"Were you raised in the Depression?"

"Vagina, the other white meat."

"Now that's just insulting. It's totally a pink meat."

"The point is you're a lesbian. We support you. I'm not saying there isn't homophobia in the world, but you were arrested because you broke into someone's house. After writing them super creepy letters. That's not being a lesbian; that's being a stalker who happens to **be** a lesbian. Normal lesbians find girls online. They get hooked up by friends. Heck, I know a couple women who'd give their left ovary for a chance at grabbing your ring. It's not normal to stalk b-list celebrities."

"Tina had the number three song on the Billboard top 100 chart last fall." I corrected Carly. "She is not b-list."

"Of all the things I just said, that is what you're gonna focus on?"

"You don't understand." I put my head on the desk and covered it with my arms.

"I understand that you're going to jail for this woman. And making a cop impotent."

I felt Carly's hand on my shoulder.

"The situation is a lot more nuanced than that." I said through the table and my arms.

"Does that 'nuance' involve drinking wine made in a prison toilet?"

There was a sudden knock on the door. I lifted my head from my arms in time to see it open enough for the detective to stick her head through.

"You have professional visitors, ladies." was all she said before letting two women enter.

The first gave off an alpha female vibe you could pick up on Mars. She was closer to fifty than forty. Tall enough to get away with flats. Not that she'd did. Her heels were long and sharp. Like the back claws of some she demon. I half expected to see a trail of blood where she walked from her last victim/lover. She wore a tailored power suit that cost more than my rent, and an expression that said she didn't give a fuck about the streaks of grey in her long black hair. Her skirt was long, but I could see enough of her legs to tell she was wearing stockings. I guessed they were stockings anyway. For some reason I wanted them to not be tights or pantyhose. She strode into the room not so much like she owned the place, but like she'd be slumming if she ever deigned to buy it.

The other woman was none of those things. The first woman looked like she was a statue of some ancient war goddess brought to life and put in a suit. The second woman … not so much. I suppose she was cute with her softer side of Sears wardrobe and that pile of wild curly hair going everywhere, but she looked more like a middle manager than a deity.

"I'm Elizabeth McCaskill." The alpha took a seat opposite me. "I represent Tina Jordan. We have a lot to talk about, Ms. Hogarth."

McCaskill didn't offer me her hand to shake. She didn't introduce the other woman. She just locked eyes with me and stared so intently that I melted a little.

"Carly Vintner, esquire." Carly was trying to sound formal, but was coming off like a small child just learning good manners. "Is it appropriate for you to be seeing my client?"

"If you don't know the answer to that question, Ms. Vintner, esquire you can go outside and Google 'things a real attorney should know.' Otherwise you can stay here while I make your client an offer she can't afford to refuse."

McCaskill didn't take her eyes from mine.

"What's your offer?" I could hear just the faintest ring of defeat in Carly's voice.

"Your client is under the delusion that she is an intimate part of my client's life." McCaskill said.

"I'm not delusional, I ..." I wanted to say more, but the alpha's stare intensified and I couldn't speak.

"Do you want to belong to Tina Jordan?" McCaskill asked.

"... yes." The way she said "belong" had a powerful effect on me

"There's a condition."

"I don't care. I'll shave my head. Wear burlap underwear. Donate a kidney. Anything Tina wants. I'll … OWWW!"

Carly had pinched my bare leg under the table.

"What conditions?" Carly asked. "And why would she even do that?"

"I'll let my companion explain those conditions." alpha said. "The why is simple. Ms. Jordan is closeted, but looking for a partner she can explore her sexuality with in a way that won't threaten her career. Against my advice she believes your client can be Pygmalioned into acceptability. And if Ms. Hogarth tries to out my client, her mental condition will make it easy to discredit her in the press."

"By strapping down her boobs and gluing on a beard? And this is the 21st century; who cares if Tina Jordan is gay?"

"The 75 million red blooded American men who imagine they might one day fuck her." McCaskill answered.

"Dudes love lesbians." Carly countered.

"Ms. Jordan doesn't want to be the kind of lesbian that dudes love."

"So you want Becky to be a secret sex slave to some diva? That is so far away from appropriate it would take the light from inappropriate two years to get to sex slave diva world."

"Let's ask your client." alpha still hadn't looked away from me. "You've been wet since I told you Tina was gay, haven't you, Becky?"

"WHAT THE FUCK!" Carly looked like she was about to have a stroke.

"You want to belong to Tina, don't you, Becky? You want to be loved and owned by her?"

"Get out of here right now you crazy bitch." Carly had gotten to her feet and was walking to the door.

"Yes." I said. "Yes to all of it. What are the conditions?"

Carly threw her hands up in the air and said something I couldn't hear, but was pretty sure was a curse word.

The alpha attorney broke eye contact with me and turned to the mousy middle manager.

"Tag. You're it."

"Hello, my name is Claire and I represent the Stovent Company."

Claire spoke for half an hour.

I think.

Frankly my head was in a swirl from the thought of being with Tina. And the condition didn't seem that bad to me. Wicked weird, but it was rapidly growing on me.

"You have an hour to say yes. After that it becomes a pumpkin and the next girlfriend you have will be your cellmate."

McCaskill rose from her seat and took Claire with her out the door.

"The number one rule of law club is this." Carly said as soon as we were alone. "If opposing counsel asks if you're wet or you want to be her client's sex slave you … don't … fucking … answer!"

"Sorry. I don't know what happened there. It wasn't even Tina being gay so much as it was her. That attorney I mean. She just stared at me with these laser eyes and I felt like I was all naked and vulnerable. And really cool with that."

"That's great, but we have to figure out what we're going to do."

"Just remembering how she so badly out lawyered you is getting me going a little. It was like you were a red headed step child and she was this sexy sexy King Kong."

"We need to focus here, cookie. What are we going to do when you say 'no?'"

"There's nothing to discuss." I said. "I"m going to accept."

"Have you gone completely bug nuts? Did you here what those mad scientists want to do to you?"

"They're going to make me Tina's little doll. Isn't that so romantic?"

"No … no. It is not romantic. Strip away all of that flowery bull-shit you're spinning my way and all you got is this – you will sign a paper taking away all of your rights. Then they will shrink you small enough to use my Princess Leia action figure as a mannequin, then Tina will buy you like a puppy from the pound only the puppy will have more legal protections than you. She will own you and there will be nothing you or I can do about it."

"I want to be owned by Tina." I said. "I'd never even heard of this shrinking company, but now that I have this is perfect. Tina is just scared that I'm going to turn out to be some sort of rando nut job. If me being helpless and tiny creates a safe space for her to get to know me for the real me I am all for that shit. And the whole power dynamic thing is much sexier than I thought it would be. I won't be her girlfriend or wife; I'll be Tina's property."

"Honey, we fought a war so that wouldn't happen again."

"No. You can't white guilt me out of this. Just tell me what I need to do next."

"I studied tax law." Carly said. "I'm in over my head representing you in a criminal case. This is bleeding edge law. You sign that contract and you legally stop being a human being. I can't even tell you how many light years away that is from what I know."

"Can you try. Please. I'm going to do this and I'd rather have someone I love and trust in my corner. Attorney sexy pants may have gotten into my head, but you're still in my heart and I really really need this. Please."

"I don't know what I can tell you. I've heard about Shrink Inc, but most of what I know is what the mad scientist's apprentice told us."

"Yeah … about that. I kinda got a little distracted when she was going through her spiel. Thinking about being Tina's little love doll. And the way McCaskill was undressing me with her scowl. I may have spaced out some of the deets."

"Some?"

"Almost all. She said I was going to be shrunk to a few inches tall and I came up with this super hot fantasy of Tina and her attorney changing my outfits and the rest was just blah blah blah."

"Jesus Christ! You can be such a dude sometimes." Carly said, turning her head to the ceiling.

"Depends on the outfit. And the accessories."

"OK. Here's what she said in a nutshell. You sign your life away then they wheel you into this room where they'll shrink you. Like really really tiny. Like Barbie will be beating you up and taking your lunch money small."

"How do they do it?"

"I don't know.

"Is it some sort of shrink ray? Or a pill?"

"I don't know."

"Or maybe all this science stuff is some sort of cover and they use dark magic."

"If they told us, they'd have to kill us." Carly said.

"Did they really say that? Cause that sounds stone cold butch."

"I'm paraphrasing. Slightly. The important thing to take away from this is it's permanent. They don't have a growth ray. Or pill. Or spell. They're Shrink Inc, not Grow Inc."

"Of course not. That would be Grow Co."

"No such thing. You get shrunk you stay that way."

"That is so hardcore." My expression may have gotten a bit distant.

"You're having more sexy fantasies about opposing counsel, aren't you?"

"... maybe."

"Then stop. I'm only going through this once."

"I'm sorry."

"Saying 'I'm sorry' and making a pouty face isn't going to get you out of this mess, Becks. This isn't like the time you stole aunt Linda's Subaru."

"OK. So I sign the papers. They shrink me. Somehow. So then they give me to Tina? I'm thinking I can be in a box of chocolates. A really nice one. Not that Russel Stovers crap you buy at the drug store either. Something classy. And I can be covered in that chocolate dip they use for ice cream. What do they call that stuff? Magic shell. I can be covered in magic shell and when Tina opens the box she can lick me till she finds my creamy center."

"I'm going to pretend that I didn't hear that." Carly said. "No. The next step is training."

"But I want to find out how many licks it takes to get to my creamy center."

"That phrase is even worse when you whine like that."

"What kind of training?" I asked.

"How not to die when you're small enough to fit in a toaster training."

"How do I do that?"

"I don't know; stay away from toasters."

"Ha ha." I dead laughed. "How long does it take? And who's the trainer? Please, please let it be sexy alpha lawyer." I crossed my fingers for luck.

"Two weeks minimum. Maybe a month. The trainer works for Stovent."

"Like Claire?" I knew I sounded disappointed.

"Or her clone."

"They have human clones? You're not just fucking with me, are you?"

"Yeah. A whole army of evil clone lawyers in fuck me pumps and laser glasses."

"That's ... horrible."

"Now you're fantasizing about a room full of dominatrix lawyers."

"OK. Let's just put my noble struggle against a domineering mob of corseted killers aside ..."

"I didn't say anything about corsets."

"Don't ruin this for me, Carly."

"Focus."

"So after the training then it's time for chocolate surprise?"

"Then there's the final meeting. It'll be Claire, Tina and you. Shrunken you. Shrunken you who will never be able to reach a door knob again. If either you or Tina change your minds then you go your separate ways. Otherwise you'll belong to that pop bitch."

"Well I'm not going to change my mind. And Tina's not going to ... unless. No. What if Tina doesn't want me? What happens then?"

"Then Stovent puts you in a human pet shop and sells you to whatever perv they want to. Even if they have a neck beard."

"But I can say no, right? If I can say no to Tina I can so no to neckbeard."

"I'm afraid not."

"Why not?"

"It's the way the law was written. You can change your mind in that one situation then you have the legal rights of an ottoman."

"But Tina isn't going to say no. It makes no sense for her to go to all this trouble so we can finally be together for her to say no at the last minute. What happens when we both say yes?"

"She drops you down the front of her underwear and you both live happily ever after."

"Really?"

"You couldn't hear the sarcasm in my voice?"

"Too busy thinking about Tina's panties."

"Listen very carefully, Becks." Carly put her hands on mine and looked me straight in the eye. "This whole Stovent thing sounds like a bad deal to me. There are a thousand ways this can go pear shaped and all of them involve your life being ruined. I know you think you love Tina, but she doesn't even know you. For all you know she'll keep you a couple months and get bored with you. Or she'll get a normal sized girlfriend and you won't be so special to her any more. Then what's going to happen? There'll be no way back to your old life. Assuming she doesn't just flush you down the toilet when it's over. Or have that bitch of a lawyer do it for her. Do you still want to go through with this?"

Two: Lower Case

"I know you said you couldn't tell us about how you shrink people, but I was thinking maybe you could just … I don't know … maybe blink twice if we guess right. Then you're not telling us, but we kinda sorta know what's going on."

"I can't do that Ms. Hogarth." Claire didn't seem too thrilled by my plan. Or maybe she was just playing it safe in case her overlords were spying on us.

"I totally understand." I said. "Is it a circle of necromancers who suck the size out of you and use it to fuel their dark magics?"

"Why don't I leave you two to go over the documents one last time while I collect Ms. Jordan's team." Claire said. "Feel free to use the Keurig."

Claire left Carly and me in an empty conference room.

"Did you see that." I said. "She blinked twice. It's totally necromancers."

"I should never have let you have that double espresso before we got on the plane." Carly took a seat and began to pour through the huge stack of papers.

The last month had been a crazy flash. After I'd said "yes" to becoming Tina's doll gal pal, charges were dropped. Carly mentioned something about the cop I'd busted getting some hush money, but the important thing was that I was out of jail and on the path towards Tina and the rest of our lives together.

All I had to do was leave my life behind. Not that it took the whole month to do that. I was 25 and hadn't really made it in the world yet. So it's not like my job was too bothered by me calling out forever. And I didn't have much family other than Carly. I posted my stuff on Craigslist and dreamed about what my life would be like as Tina's little doll. I ended up going through a lot of batteries and a lot of web searches. I had a lot of time on my hands and nothing better to do than figuring out the mating habits of shrunken folks. And fap to them.

There are a lot of very creative, very perverted people out there on the internet.

God bless 'em.

I wanted to belong to Tina right then and there, but it takes time making the mountain of paperwork that Carly was still going through.

I was worse than a kid waiting for Christmas and her birthday combined. I know I drove Carly insane, but I'm in love and that sorta comes with the territory.

It felt weird getting on the plane with just the clothes on my back and my purse. No carryon. No bags to check. I didn't need them. I was going someplace where someone else was going to take care of all my needs. It was a little scary, but also comforting. I hadn't even met Tina yet (although I totally knew her from her songs, her interviews, and the podcast) and I was already giving up all of my control to her. She could dress me in silks and satins or a raggy ripped up pair of her period panties and I'd have no other choice. I felt like a princess out of the Arabian Nights being brought to her new mistress. It was romantic and sexy and a little unsettling.

"Is that a new dress?" Carly asked looking up from the papers.

"Yes. Do you think Tina will like it?"

I spread the long skirt out and did a twirl for my cousin. Unlike her I was way too wired to sit down and read.

"Tina's barely going to see you in it."

"It's the exact shade of navy blue as the one she wore to the Golden Globe Awards this year."

"And in an hour you will never fit into it again."

"You don't think the cleavage is too much do you?" I asked leaning forward. "I'm going for 'freaky yet classy' and I'm worried this might be a bit too classy."

"It's not."

"Thank you. I got new undies too." I said. "I was super torn. I know I'm supposed to wear dark lingerie with a dress this color, but I wanted to wear white for Tina. You know kind of a first time virginal thing."

"Didn't need to know any of that."

There was a knock on the door followed by Claire walking in followed by McCaskill and a pair of orderlies in scrubs.

"Let's get this over with." McCaskill said, taking a seat opposite Carly.

"Where's Tina?" I asked. "Shouldn't we wait for her to get here?"

"Ms. Jordan won't be attending this meeting." Claire explained. "Ms. McCaskill is authorized to sign her portion of the required paperwork."

"But I thought ..."

"That was your first mistake." McCaskill cut me off. "You'll meet Ms. Jordan after your training is over, Becky. The sooner we get this out of the way, the sooner you'll get to roll over for your new owner."

"... uh … ok." I hadn't signed anything yet, but I already felt like the smallest person in the room.

"You don't have to do this." Carly whispered in my ear. I hadn't even seen her get up from the table I was so focused on McCaskill. "Going to jail isn't as bad as what they're going to do to you."

"Tina's going to give me a home and love me and take care of me."

Carly's face showed how sad and disappointed she was. "Let's get you started then." Was all she said as she led me to the stack of papers I had to sign.

"Maybe … instead of signing all this complicated legal mumbo jumbo you can just shrink me and I can live with Tina as her tiny gal pal. Sort of a Stuart Little thing where I get my own adorable little car and my own little clothes."

"That's not how this works, Ms. Hogarth." Claire said. "The law doesn't allow you to remain autonomous and be resized."

"Start signing." McCaskill said. I know she didn't put the pen in my hand, but it felt like she had.

By the time I'd reached the bottom of the stack my hand was cramping worse than a sorority on the wrong weekend. I pushed the final page across the table to McCaskill and watched her sign me into slavery. My stomach was doing flip flops as I realized there was no going back now. They hadn't shrunk me, but I wasn't a person any more.

"Miss Vintner, esquire, you no longer have a client here." McCaskill said. "Just a piece of property that doesn't belong to you. You will leave now."

"I'm going to miss you, cookie."

Carly was crying when she put her arms around me and hugged me for the last time. Her emotions were so overwhelming they started to leak out into me and I felt myself start to bawl as well. I think I told her goodbye, but it was so intense I can't say for sure.

It took us a minute to pull ourselves apart, but we managed to before anyone called security. I waved limply as Carly walked out the door for the last time.

"Come over here." McCaskill ordered. It took a second for it to register that she was talking to me.

"I want you to stand in front of me with your hands at your sides."

I dabbed my eyes with a tissue and obeyed. She'd pulled her chair out from the table so there was nothing between her and me. Nothing to hide behind. Nothing to protect me. She motioned me to stop when I was maybe five feet in front of her.

"Turn around." she ordered.

I did, but was ordered to do it again "slower."

I was aware of every one in the room looking at me in my new dress that I'd bought with a credit card that now wouldn't work. The eyes of strangers looking at my body like I was some sexualized cow being judged for market.

I felt myself getting aroused despite myself.

"Lose the dress." McCaskill said in a no-nonsense way that made me feel tinglier than I want to admit.

"You'll have to buy me dinner first." I smiled trying to sell my joke. Everything was way too serious.

"I bought you."

"Wellll. Technically that isn't true. Not yet anyway. I have to go through Tina survival training then we both have to pick up our options to buy. Then Tina will own me. I'm a little unclear why I should drink your cool aid."

"You'll do what I tell you to do because I know you want to be Tina's. You're going to pick up that option. Piss me off and I'll tell Ms. Jordan that you're not worth it and she'll turn you down. Then I will do everything in my power to make certain that the person who buys you is the last person you want to belong to. I know a gun nut who's been trying to sell the NRA on a sexually explicit adult out- reach program. He just needs a tiny woman to straddle a hot gun barrel naked and oiled. I'm not sure if any of that was a euphemism, but you're free to keep the dress on and find out."

"Are you threatening me, McCaskill?"

"I didn't mean to turn you on." she gave me a smile the Chesire Cat would have found smug.

"I … I am not." I said, looking away from her so she couldn't see how badly I was lying. "I'll just get out of this dress then."

"Good girl." McCaskill's condescending tone should have pissed me off, but it was only throwing gasoline on my lady fire.

I don't know how much McCaskill's mind games were effecting me, but I was feeling performance pressure as I reached back to undo the tie at the back of my dress. I'd need to undo it then pull the zipper down if I wanted to shimmy out of my new frock. But my fingers had mutated into Vienna sausages and the damn knot wasn't coming undone.

"Do you need any help with that, Becky?" McCaskill asked. "I'm sure the orderlies would be happy to help if you asked real nice."

"No … I'm good. It's just that I was expecting Tina to be the one taking it off me. But it is totally a one woman job. I got it. It's all me. See – I got it."

The tie was untied. Unzipping the zip was awkward, but after a couple tries and a few contortions I didn't know my body was capable of it came down all the way. I slid the silk dress down over my hips and let it glide to the floor where it puddled at my feet.

> "Whenas in silks my Julia goes,
> Then, then (methinks) how sweetly flows
> That liquefaction of her clothes."

I daintily stepped out of the dress wearing nothing but my heels, bra, and spanx. I gave a low bow and mock curtsey as I recited my poem.

"That's 17th century for 'panty drop.' You know cause the clothes make a puddle on the floor. Puddle. Liquefaction. Get it."

I thought McCaskill was going to give me another immediate order, but she just stared at me. Through me really. Like she could see past the lingerie and the poetry and all the defense mechanisms I'd built up. I couldn't tell if she approved of what she saw or was making a mental list of my flaws. Years of being me told me to bet on the latter. I found my hands awkwardly reaching up to protect my modesty.

"Hands down." McCaskill ordered, her voice calm and smoky.

I remembered the other three people in the room. The other sets of eyes roaming over my body. I didn't even know the names of two of them.

"Pick up the dress." McCaskill ordered. For some reason she was the only other person speaking.

I did.

"Find the tag."

I did.

"Put your lips on the tag and kiss it."

"What?"

"This is the last piece of human clothing you will ever wear, Becky. You are going to kiss it good bye. Literally. I want to see that pretty red lipstick you're wearing on the tag."

"Can't you just shrink the dress too? It's so pretty and I want Tina to see me in it and it's almost brand new."

"I'm sure my friend will have no problem oiling up his gun."

Back to that threat.

I bent down, conscious of how much cleavage I was flashing Mc-Caskill and brought the dress to my face. If I hadn't felt self conscious standing around a group of strangers in my sexy underwear I'd meant to share with the love of my life I was now. I pressed my lips against the mostly white tag and kissed reverently. I looked at the red marks I'd made on it. It was a pretty red.

"Put the dress on the table and take off your bra. Once the bra is off I expect you to keep your hands at your sides unless ordered otherwise. Remember, you signed away your modesty."

I unsnapped my bra and let it slide down my arms. McCaskill hadn't been specific about what to do with it so I just held it in my hand at my side.

"Sure is chilly in here." I thought that a bad joke might make me feel less embarrassed about how painfully erect my nipples were. Not just from the cold.

"Walk over to the table. Find your lip stick in your purse and apply a heavy coat."

I had a sinking feeling I knew where this was going.

Normally I don't think about how my boobs move when I'm topless. I mean I can feel them trying to strike off in their own directions, but I've had them since I was fourteen so I'm kinda used to them having a mind of their own. Unless I'm giving myself a pair of black eyes by jogging topless I don't pay them much attention.

But normally I'm not prancing around in nothing but high heels and the sexiest spanx my Visa gold card could afford in front of a middle manager and two bored orderlies while being ordered around by middle aged dominatrix Barbie. Each bonce they made made me feel just a little dirtier in a way my head was having trouble processing. It was humiliating, erotic, and scary all at the same time.

Putting something phallic shaped up to my lips to make them look more like my vajayjay was a cakewalk after that. Even applying the second and third coats that McCaskill insisted on. I'm pretty sure I looked like I walked out of a Robert Palmer video. If the dancers had curves. And went topless.

"We might allow you a doll brassiere, but this is the last human bra you will ever wear. You'll kiss it goodbye also. Two kisses. On the inside. Right where your nipple rested. Like you were suckling your own teat."

"I can't do that." I looked around the room. Claire was looking at her laptop. The orderlies still looked bored.

"And you will tell me what it feels like."

"... no." I said with even less conviction. By now it was obvious that McCaskill got what she wanted.

McCaskill didn't say a word as she rose up out of her chair. Her expression was neutral, but I still felt deeply intimidated by this fully clothed woman who towered a full head taller than me.

How much scarier would she be when she could fit me in the palm of her hand?

She reached up and cupped one of my breasts in her hand. I felt a flash of pleasure followed by a swell of dumb pride at the fact she couldn't fit my whole boob in one hand. As small as I was destined to become, right now I was still too much woman for the alpha attorney to handle.

Then she squeezed and any illusion of power I might have fantasized about disappeared like a fist when you open your hand. As painful as it was I still held my ground, refusing to lower myself to kiss my own bra.

Then she dug her nails into my tender boobs.

"Stop stop stop Uncle I'll do it." I whined as I danced around trying to distract myself from the agony radiating from my chest.

McCaskill held on for another ten seconds then let go. My poor tit throbbed in pain as the blood started to flow back.

"You really are a very pretty girl." McCaskill said, running her hands through my hair. "It's a shame we have to shrink you."

"Wait … wha?"

"No more questions." McCaskill quieted me by placing two fingers close to my mouth. "Just obey me and everything will be all right."

"Yes, Ma'am."

McCaskill took the lipstick from my other hand. Now I could hold the bra in both shaking hands as I debased myself in front of her.

I brought the white lace cups to my face and all I could think of was how stupid I felt about to kiss my own bra like I was some sort of introverted narcissistic perv who got off on her own tits. I found the spot in the cup where my stiff nipple had been pressed. I could just barely see the indentation I'd made in the fresh fabric. I brought my too red lips down on it and kissed.

"Tell me what you're feeling."

"Stupid. Humiliated."

"Tell me more."

"I don't know what you want me to tell you." I stared into the white fabric unwilling to acknowledge any world beyond it.

"Is it still warm? Can you still feel the heat of your breast?"

"Yes."

"Can you still smell yourself on it?"

"Yes."

"What do you smell like?"

"Talcum powder. Lilacs. Sweat."

"Do you like how you smell?"

I paused before answering "yes."

"So do I."

I felt a gentle pressure on my breast followed by something cold. It took me a second to realize that McCaskill was running the tip of the lipstick over the engorged nipple. She was painting my nipple with the same lip stick I'd run across my lips minutes before. I was kissing an object that had touched my nipple while something that had touched my lips was kissing my teat.

"You're only halfway done." McCaskill said.

I lifted my face. Looking down I could see a perfect lip stick kiss in the center of that cup. Pretty. Feminine. Mine. I moved my face the few inches I needed to in order to line up my second kiss goodbye. As I planted it McCaskill took my breast into her warm mouth. I pressed my lips into the waiting cup as my future owner ran her tongue over my sensitive flesh.

I held the kiss until she was finished with me. Her mouth left my body. I could feel her still warm breath begin to dry the layer of saliva she'd left behind. When I lifted my face from my bra she was staring directly into my eyes.

"The next time I take you in my mouth it won't just be one breast, it will be all of you. Now take off that girdle." She punctuated her order with a spank to my spanx covered butt.

"I don't think I've ever been this wet before in my entire life. And I've just spent the last month pretty much just fapping off to size porn."

It took me a second to realize that I'd said that last part out loud, but by then I didn't care what anyone thought.

I pulled the spanx down as quickly as I could. But they were pretty tight fitting foundation wear so "quickly" was a relative term. It was a small miracle I didn't fall over in my heels as I pulled and prodded them down my legs and onto the floor.

I expected McCaskill to make me kiss them too. That would be even more humbling than the bra. I reached down deep trying to find the strength to say no to that, but mostly I thought about how much more fun it would be to just go with the flow and obey.

But she didn't.

Instead she put my lipstick back in my purse, picked the spanx off the floor, and pushed the purse and folded up bra into my dazed hands.

"Little Becky's ready to be resized." McCaskill said to Claire before turning her attention back to me. I felt her hand rest on my bare butt. "Now be a good little girl while Claire and I discuss your training and any optional procedures I might want done to you."

"Wait. No one said anything abo..."

McCaskill shut me up with one long deep kiss that took my brain away. It lasted at least two centuries and when it ended her mouth was covered in my lipstick.

"Move along, Becky. The grownups have a lot to talk about."

McCaskill patted me on the butt to move me along. In my stupor I let the orderlies maneuver me out the door. The last time I saw Elizabeth McCaskill, while I was still human height, she was wiping my lipstick off her lips with my dirty underwear.

"So that was a head trip, huh?"

I was walking down a long shiny corridor clutching the purse and bra that McCaskill had pushed into my hands against my otherwise naked boobs. It wasn't for modesty so much as comfort; the orderlies who were taking me to see the Wizard had seen everything I had and hadn't seemed especially impressed.

The click clack of my high heels echoed on the polished floor. They were the only other things I had with me and the only clothing I was technically wearing. I suppose I could have slipped the bra back on, but after all that drama back in the office it would have felt weird putting my kiss marks on my nipples. Besides they'd probably just take it off before they put me through the smallifying machine.

"Yeah, but don't worry. We've seen it all before." the lady orderly said. "Most future owners want to put on a little bit of a show for their subs. Give them a real experience they're never going to forget."

"I'm not a sub." I said.

"A ha."

"I can see where you'd think that what with all the … everything, but, seriously I'm more of a switch."

"Lady, you're about to become too small to top a Go Bot." the man orderly said. I didn't like man orderly.

"I'm not saying it won't be a challenge exerting my female power at that size, but I think that life is about overcoming obstacles." I said. "And McCaskill isn't my future owner; she works for my future owner. Tina Jordan, pop superstar. McCaskill is sorta my … well, girl crush isn't the right word. I mean she's old enough to be my mother so calling her girl sounds weird. Can girls get Oedipus complexes?"

"Speaking of sounding weird." lady orderly said.

"Enough about that. What happens now?"

"Now we bring you down to processing and they resize you." lady orderly said.

"McCaskill mentioned something about optional procedures. Sounds a little ominous."

"It is." man orderly the jerk said.

"Your prospective owner might have a special request for how you come out once you're resized." lady orderly offered. "Most of that stuff is easier to do before or during the resizing."

"What kind of requests?"

"Permanent hair removal is a pretty popular one." lady orderly said.

"Making the subject mute's up there too. They say it makes the resized feel more like a pet if they can't talk back."

"And there was that one woman who they made permanently lactate. I have no idea what that was about."

"People are weird."

"Do you think they'll do any of that to me?" I asked.

"Probably." man orderly said.

"What?"

"Liposuction. Lots of it."

Man orderly had been instantly upgraded from dislike to hate when he made a point of staring at my ass when he said that.

"Now look here mister shrinker man. I am border line … border line zaftig. I do not need to lose weight."

"Well you're going to whether you need to or not."

"Over 99% of it." lady orderly finished.

"But they couldn't do anything like that without my permission. Could they?"

"It's so cute when they think they're people."

I was brought into a huge white room filled with a metric butt ton of science stuff and a half dozen necromancers in mad scientist drag. I mean they had lab coats, but I could totally smell sulphur. And maybe brimstone. Though I have to admit I'm a little shaky about what exactly brimstone smells like.

The leader of the coven walked up to me with her hands out. I used one hand to hold my things to my chest while I awkwardly shook one of her hands.

"Rebecca Hogarth. I'll be your victim today."

She pulled her hand away from mine and reached for my stuff instead.

"Right. You probably need to check that. Or something."

She walked off without acknowledging me.

Another "scientist" came over and began poking and prodding me, but I couldn't get her to respond either. No matter how witty my banter got. After several minutes I was laid out on a table. I felt my shoes being taken off. I hoped my feet didn't smell to rank.

It wasn't until they put the needle in my arm that the full weight of what I was doing came crashing in on me. All the things I had signed away. All the things I was about to lose. I wasn't ready for this. Maybe I'd never be ready for this. Carly was right. I didn't want this.

"... I don't want to be a doll." I said, but my voice was too small for even me to hear.

Then everything went black.

Three: Out of the Training Bra ...

"I don't feel any smaller."

I was slowly pushing through the necromancers' sleep spell and my eyes were still closed. Every time I opened them before it ended up being a dream. And not a the fun sexy kind either. I remembered flashes of Carly, Tina, and McCaskill cutting me up into little pieces. Another where the mad scientists hooked up my intestines to a plastic extruder and they ran off thousands of little plastic tubes through me. I didn't want to be fooled again, but I really thought I was awake for real this time.

I could tell I was still naked without having to open my eyes. And I felt cleaner than I had before I was laid out on that table. My makeup was definitely gone. Which was probably a good thing considering the tears and what happened after the tears.

Had someone bathed me? The thought of some stranger washing me was creeping me out. The idea that it might have been in a bathroom sink only made it weirder.

I wasn't on the table anymore. Whatever it was I was laying on was made of a very soft fabric that was very yielding. Like a hammock. Only it must have been a huge one since I couldn't feel the edge with my hands.

I could see light coming from above me through my closed lids. It didn't feel warm like sunlight would, but it was probably pretty bright.

"OK. I'm opening my eyes. If this is another nightmare I am going to be royally pissed."

I had to squint at first. The light was a bit much, but my eyes adjusted after a couple minutes and a few hundred blinks. I couldn't look up without getting blinded, but I was able to get a pretty good look at myself and my immediate surroundings.

I looked like me. At least as far as I could see of me without a mirror. And I had talked earlier. If they'd made any alterations to me I couldn't tell. Even my size. Like I said, I didn't feel any smaller. And I didn't wake up with a giant tarantula crouched over me. As far as I was concerned I was still 5'3" and this whole thing was a huge hoax.

I still wasn't sure what I was laying on. It was all made out of the same super soft white material I was laying on. It was round. Ish. Like an upside down igloo. Made of silk. It was maybe twenty feet across and the upper edge was ten. There was some sort of rigid piping running under maybe half of the edge. Like a curved tent pole. Thanks to the light I couldn't get a real good look at was outside the bowl shaped super hammock I was resting on.

"Hello! Is there anybody out there? I'm not making a Pink Floyd reference, I'm just trying to figure out what the fuck happened to me."

Nothing.

"That's ok. I'll find my own way out of this super freaky hammock thing."

Getting up wasn't as easy as I'd hoped it would be. Whatever this fabric was it was almost as unsteady as a normal hammock. There were more than one failed attempts. I finally managed to pull my legs under me while resting my arms on the "ground" for support. I slowly pushed myself up with my feet while using my arms for balance. I'd almost made it all the way up when I caught a flash of red out of the corner of my eye. At first I thought it was blood. That they'd done something surgical to me like take out my kidney and didn't bother stitching me up again or putting me in a bathtub full of ice.

Then I realized what it really was.

"FUCK!"

I came tumbling down to the ground. I managed to avoid face planting in the silk by putting my arm out to cover me. It ended up lined up parallel to one of the two red lines on the white fabric. A curved line that was longer than my forearm.

"My pretty red lipstick kiss."

I knelt there for a good long time taking that in.

"Hey! Something went wrong. I wasn't supposed to get this small."

No response.

"A little help here. I'm trapped in my own god damned bra. And I really need to pee."

Still nothing.

"This better be a nightmare."

But I knew it wasn't. I could smell the powder and the lilac and the sweat and I knew this was real and that I was going to have to get myself out of this. Like some super pervy after school special.

This time I managed to stand up. The top of my head was barely halfway to the top. There was enough lateral space for three more of me to fit comfortably. I couldn't be this small. I couldn't be so tiny that I didn't even measure up to one of my normal sized breasts.

My best chance was to climb the underwire side and use it to pull myself out. I imagined myself doing this complex Scarlet Johansson parkour complete with a leg kick/back flip combination to get me over the top.

I started to make my move, but I didn't have enough momentum and my feet were sliding on the shifting surface beneath me. I made a final lunge to grab the underwire, but missed by two feet and sliding all the way down to my lipstick mark.

"Maybe I'm dead." I said, feeling the sting of a bra burn across the entire front of my body. "Maybe I'm dead and this is big boobed woman hell. Spending the rest of eternity trying to get out of your own damn bra."

I gave myself a minute before standing up again. I tried not to think about the fact that my foot was pressing down exactly where my nipple had been resting only a few hours ago. Talk about feeling diminished.

This time I knew how the material was going to shift under my weight. I had a better idea about how fast I'd need to run to get up the slope before I became gravity's bitch. This time I was going to do it. I pulled my chin down, took a couple steps back to help with momentum, and raced as fast as I could.

I nailed the speed. And I was dead on about how the bra was going to shift under me. I had everything figured out except how running uphill as fast as I could, naked, was really going to work out for me. With my chin tucked in close to my chest.

My right boob hit me first. It hurt, but mostly I felt the shock of my own boob slapping me in the cheek. By the time my left boob followed through I was already falling backwards. I managed to land on my butt right back at the lipstick starting line.

"Is this supposed to be some sort of O. Henry story? If I was wearing my bra I could get out of my bra. Really? On top of big boobed woman hell?"

If I held my breasts down I wouldn't have them for balance. Or to grab the underwire when I got up there. If I ever got up there. I wasn't going to be able to parkour my way out. No one was listening to me.

There was only one thing left for me to try.

I got on all fours. Like an animal. I hated being in this position. Especially when I was naked. I love my breasts and I love my body, but it feels so weird to have my boobs just hang straight down like that. There's a reason why people don't walk on all fours. Two legs is human. Four is animal. And with my breasts dangling down below me

I felt like a cow. A cow with huge dry udders.

I reached out and gripped the material hard and pulled myself a few inches closer to the top.

It was slow going pulling myself forward on my hands and knees. Crawling out of my bra like a mouse. No. Not a mouse. Like a butterfly almost ready to emerge from her chrysalis who does something stupid and crawls out a caterpillar.

I should have listened to you, Carly.

It took a long time, but my hand finally groped the underwire. I pulled myself up and onto the flat hard surface beyond. I pulled myself to my feet to preserve whatever dignity I could and looked around.

I was in a room. A giant room. I tried to focus on specific objects, but they were all so far away and there was a light tower pointed at me that made it even harder to see.

"Congratulations," the light tower said. "you got out of your bra all by yourself. You must feel like such a big girl."

I stared up at the light on the tower where the giant lady voice came from. Speakers. It had to be speakers. Otherwise it meant that this was really happening and this couldn't be really happening cause if this was really happening it meant that I had royally screwed the pooch. Only it wasn't a light on the top of the tower; it was a phone with its light pointed down recording me. And it wasn't a light tower it was a woman. A humungous giant woman who I had never seen before. Only that didn't matter cause her phone was bigger than me. Like the biggest big screen TV I'd ever seen and she was just waving it around like it was nothing to her. Which meant that I was nothing to her. Which meant she was going to kill me.

"Submissive urination, that's a new one." the giant lady said, taking the phone away from her dark face. She looked younger than me.

It was like one of those nightmares where you're so scared you can't move even though every drop of blood in your skull is screaming at you to just run away. My brain no longer sent signals to my body. It was receiving just fine. I could feel the cool air on my bare skin. I could feel the hot liquid cascade down my legs and puddle at my feet. But I couldn't send the order to move out of the puddle and away from the giant reality staring me in the tiny face.

This wasn't possible. I know what I'd been told, but there was a part of me that never really believed it. People don't just get turned into toys. I was expecting Ashton Kutcher to step out and tell me I'd been Punk'd. That they were just looking to catch me on film fapping to size porn and peeing myself.

This was impossible.

"You look like you've totally checked out." the impossible woman said. "That's cool. Vermin like you always freak out when you see a real person for the first time. It's not your fault. There's only so much you can process at one time. Like bladder control and dealing with a giant talking to you. It's going to take some time getting used to having a smaller brain."

"Nobody said anything about getting dumber. I am not dumber. Do you think I'm dumb?" my body may not be picking up what my brain was laying down, but my mouth sure was.

"It's not your fault. Right now your brain is basically the size of a dinosaur's. And you know what happened to them. Or maybe not. Cause of the pea brain."

"Look, Giganta, I am just as smart as I was before."

"I'm sure people say the same thing after their lobotomies. But that's ok. All you need to know is that I'm Lauren. Can you say 'LAUREN?'"

"Seriously?" I asked, cause she couldn't be.

She just stared down at me without saying anything.

"OK. Yes. I can say 'Lauren.' Does that make you happy?"

"I love it when I teach vermin new tricks. It makes me feel complete as a woman."

"First off, take the sarcasm down a skosh, LAUREN. Second, what's up with vermin? My name is Rebecca. Ms. Hogarth if you're nasty."

"This is amazing." the giant woman said. "Your body is rigid in terror. You're frozen in a puddle of your own pee. But you're talking like I couldn't just slam my phone down on top of you and turn you into a silent stain. Guess you aren't as smart as you think you are."

Lauren held her phone up over me. For her it was only a few ounces held a couple feet above some vermin; for me it was as heavy as a piano dangling seventy feet above me.

"Do you have anything else to say, vermin?" she asked me.

"...no..."

"I'm your trainer. In the next few weeks I need to turn you into the best pet you can possibly be. Pets are trained. Vermin aren't. Pets are obedient and quiet. Vermin aren't. Pets are housebroken. Vermin aren't. I hope you have it in you to become a pet, but until then you're just vermin."

I stood there feeling my own pee squish between my toes as a woman I had never met before. A woman who looked barely twenty. Explained that I was beneath pets on my new social ladder and maybe, just maybe, she was going to bring me up to their level if I wasn't too dumb.

You were so right, Carly.

Lauren lowered the phone. Wicked fast. I thought she was slamming it down. Probably on me. But she ended up laying it on the other side of the table from where I was cowering. I was relieved not to be start my new life over again as a stain, but not so relieved that I didn't notice she put it down gently. She must have been pushing that phone a hundred miles an hour, but it barely made a sound when she placed it on the table. Then she turned and walked across the giant room.

There's a part of me that still refused to accept that I was the one who changed. A part of me that didn't so much think that I had shrunk so much as the rest of the world had grown. To that part of me Lauren must have weighed tons and towered over me like a snarky office building. I don't want to sound like I'm profiling, but she looked like she should be lumbering around in semi-slo mo like some actor in a Godzilla suit.

But that's not how she moved. To me it looked like she was moving redonkulously fast, moving that huge body a quarter mile in less than a second with a fluid grace that I'd expect from a dancer. It had all the awe and majesty of watching a whale break the surface combined with the beauty and grace of an angel. Like they'd somehow stuffed an angel whale into a loose fitting pair of jeans, sneakers, and an old Metallica t-shirt and sent it out to pick up a paper towel.

Then the angel whale turned and headed back to where I was crossing dozens of yards with each footstep. My eyes focused on the paper towel she was holding in her right hand. It might as well have been the white sail of a tall ship. Before I'd taken in all of Lauren's giant magnificence; now all I could see was a giant hand and a huge swath of white coming to get me.

I don't know why I ran.   I didn't even know that I was running until my foot slipped on the cooling liquid I was standing in. I went tumbling down and forward managing to catch myself before I went face first in my own pee. My hands and knees splashed down in it throwing bits of it into my face and hair, but it could have been worse. Whatever lizard part of my brain that had flipped on didn't give me the time to ick over it. Animal terror propelled me forward and out of the puddle before I had time to fall any further into it.

Lauren's giant shadow fell over me as I ran naked and covered in my own filth like the vermin she said I was. I couldn't judge distance. The scale of what I could see was too alien. I didn't dare look back to see how far I'd gotten from my little yellow puddle.

Lauren's shadow grew darker as more of her got between me and the overhead light. By the time she'd eclipsed almost all the light I felt a pain in my side from trying to breathe too fast. When the light was completely gone I heard a loud swooshing sound then a giant hand swooped down and grabbed me like a bald eagle dive bombing a baby carriage.

Everything went crazy. The world just stopped making sense as I tried to process images of an insanely large world as I was being yanked upward faster than any rollercoaster towards Lauren's billboard sized face.

That's when I threw up.

"Ewwww."

Lauren's billboard sized expression was pure disgust. For me it was like the face of God was looking straight down at me and telling me that picking me up was a step down from grabbing a fresh dog turd off the ground.

"I have a tender tummy." I said turning my head away from her huge face.

I don't know why, but I felt like I'd done something wrong. OK. So puking isn't really an ideal thing to do, but it happens. Especially when someone just decides to pick you up and manhandle you like that. I knew that it wasn't my fault, but I felt like I had let Lauren down.

I wiped the last bit of sick from my chin and tried not to think about the pee my hands had fallen on.

Lauren moved with the same crazy speed. The world turned inside out again and the next thing I knew I was laying face up on cold flat metal. Some of it was grating that ran from the base of my neck to the top of my butt. There was the sound of metal grinding on metal. A giant hand swiveled something large and metal that looked way too much like a cannon, directly over my head. The hand disappeared followed by more metal grinding then the thunderclap sound of running water then my face was being blasted by a high pressure fire hose.

I turned my face to the side and tried to push my way out of the stream, but the pressure had me pinned down. I felt a giant hand reach down from above and move my flailing body around. Flipping me over and back. Making sure that every inch of me was blasted by the concentrated waterfall.

Then the hand pulled back into the sky, there was a sound of metal grinding, and the water stopped.

I was drenched. My hair was either plastered to the side of my head or wetly dangling in front of my face. I shivered there on the cool wet metal, running my hands along my body for warmth and to wipe off a little of the water that clung to my goosebumps. I curled my legs to my chin and wrapped my arms around them. Partly for warmth. Partly because I was feeling very vulnerable and exposed.

"You are in a sink under the faucet." Lauren's voice echoed down and around the metal sink. "It wasn't turned on all the way. If it was you'd probably be bleeding internally right now. I'm not telling you that to make you feel weak or pathetic. Cause I'm pretty sure you figured that out already. I'm telling you because you need to know just how dangerous the world can be for a resized. Things you used to take for granted can now maim or even kill you. Do you understand?"

"... yes ..."

I was too stunned and shivering to run when reached for me again. And it's not like there was anywhere I could run to. It was like being trapped at the bottom of an empty swimming pool without a ladder. If Lauren didn't get me out of here, I wouldn't get out of here.

Lauren held me in her hand for a minute while she fumbled around with a drawer that must have been bigger than my apartment. I pushed myself deep into her palm trying to pull out as much warmth as I could.

Then I was wrapped in something soft warm and white. It was probably just a face cloth, but at my size it was the largest comfiest towel in the world. The Guinness people needed to get on this.

Giant fingers ran the towel over me drying and warming my tiny body. Then they were gone and I found myself standing on the same table I had been on earlier with the towel wrapped completely around my body. Only my face poked out through a small hole. I let myself fall backwards onto my butt. The thick towel absorbed the impact. Not that there would have been much of one; I weighed next to nothing now.

I fought against this feeling of comfort. Lauren was a crazy bitch who had called me names and tortured me. I shouldn't feel grateful when she showed me basic human kindness. Was this what Stockholm Syndrome felt like? Or was Lauren right and there really was something wrong with my brain now that it was so much tinier. I didn't feel any different. Not mentally at least. But would I be able to tell?

Lauren crossed her arms flat on the table and rested her head on them with her ginormous face pointed right at me.

"I'm not mad at you." Lauren started, sounding every bit like a parent talking down to their kid. "It's ok that you ran. To you I'm big and scary. It's natural for you to run away. That's what vermin do. They run when they see people. I'm going to help you overcome your instinctual fear of humans. Make it so you're still aware of what we can do to you, but not running off in a blind panic every time you see one of us."

She was doing so good there for awhile. She sounded like a real person who cared. Then she got back on the vermin script and I wanted to cry or bash my head against the stone table I was sitting on.

"Look, Lauren." I tried to sound reasonable as I huddled there for warmth and dryness in my Guinness record towel. "I know they must be paying you a ton of money to get me ready for Tina and I would never stand between another woman and her true calling, but maybe we can put the whole vermin/mistress thing on the back burner. Maybe think of this as a scientific collaboration. A sisterhood of science. You seem like a good person. When you're not spouting out what other people tell you to."

"I never made you call me Mistress."

"Out of all that, that's what you're taking away?"

"I never said that word. You did."

"Not per se, but that is totally the vibe you're giving off."

"I get it. You're trying to top from the bottom. You want to call me Mistress that's fine with me. But I better hear that capital M each time or Mistress Lauren will punish you so bad."

"No no no. I don't want that. You're twisting my words around. I want to call you Lauren and you can call me Becky."

Lauren smiled a knowing smile.

"You want me to force you. I'm picking up what you're laying down. I had this boyfriend once who couldn't get it up unless I 'made' him wear my dirty panties and called him Greta. I can do that for you too. Minus the panties and the Greta part. But I can totally make you call me Mistress Lauren."

"I'm trying to take this to a higher level, Lauren."

"Exactly."

"Glad to see we're on the same wavelength then."

"You need me to take this to the next level. Make you do the things you secretly dream about. Be the mean bitch goddess you fantasized about since you first knew that being shrunk made you horny. OK, vermin, call me Mistress Lauren and I'll give my little slave a carrot."

"That's not … no … carrot?" My frustration was getting in the way of complete sentences.

"When a human, like me, wants to make a dumb animal, like you, do something the animal doesn't want to do the human can either give it a yummy carrot or a hurty stick. The carrot is a reward ...."

"And the stick is punishment. I know. I know. It's a common expression and I'm not a complete moron."

"Just enough of one to have yourself get shrunk then piss all over yourself."

I didn't have an answer to that. Not one that I wanted to give her. Not with the way I'd been kicking myself over how dumb it was to do this. Prison was looking better and better with each new humiliation I faced.

"It would be easy to just 'stick' you into submission. I could be a tenth my size and still be way bigger and stronger than you. But I think that's what you want. You resizeds get off on this sort of stuff. Having giantesses grind you into the ground until you toe the line. So I'm going to 'carrot' you into this.

"Besides. I want you to see that Mistress Lauren can be a benevolent goddess."

Lauren lifted her head and arms off the table and reached under it. After a couple minutes of scrounging around she pulled up a hand bag the size of a small house and placed it on the table a dozen feet from where I huddled in my towel.

"I've got a nummy carrot in here. One that I know you're just going to love. Call me Mistress Lauren and I'll let you have it."

"That's my purse." I said.

"You are **so** smart." Lauren's snark tipped the scale at eleven.

"What could I possibly have in there that would motivate me to call you something I will never call you?"

"The way you say 'never.' It's like you're taunting me. Will it be better for you after I make you do the thing you'd never do? Will you get a little hornier, a little wetter, knowing that you drew a line and I marched right over it?"

"I meant what I said and I said what I meant."

"Cute." Lauren said, and started rummaging in my purse. "What kind of lesbian needs birth control pills?"

Lauren tossed the half used prescription onto the table.

"The kind of lesbian who really really hates periods."

"You seriously put a bunch of synthetic hormones in your body just to skip your period?"

"Don't give me that hippie crap. Periods are Mother Nature's bad practical jokes. What's to like about them? The mess. The randomness. The bloating. The cramps. The emotional rollercoaster. The only good thing they do is tell you you're not pregnant and I got that covered by not sleeping with guys."

"Jeez." Lauren said, letting the matter drop.

She rooted around through it for a minute before finding whatever it was she was searching for. It took her several seconds to get it into position before she pulled her hand out. She was wearing a piece of thick pink plastic on the end of her index finger. It was thick, almost bulbous, at the end tapering off to firmly hug the finger at the knuckle.

"My clitoral stimulator." I didn't like the direction this was going.

Four: ...And Into The Thong

"When was the last time you used this little cutie?" Lauren waggled the huge vibrator at me like she was inviting me to a XXX puppet show.

"On the plane ride here. In the bathroom. I was thinking about … you know … Tina." I admitted. "Don't give me that slut shame face. There is nothing wrong with having a healthy libido. Or for a woman to take her pleasure in her own hand."

"Speaking of which."

Lauren's non-sex toy hand darted out and pulled me out of the comfort of the giant towel. Everything became another crazy blur as I was moved at ridiculous speeds. And my tummy. Let's just say it was a good thing it was empty.

When the world stopped spinning I was straddling the pink plastic.

"You look like a little cowgirl sitting on her saddle. I bet you can't wait for this rodeo to get started."

"This is not a good idea, Lauren."

"You are absolutely right, my little Buffalo Gal. I can't just turn this thing on and expect you to get all gooey. No. You're going to need something else. But what?"

"How about nothing. Seriously, I can take care of myself. Been doing it for years. Founding member of Players With Yourself Club."

"Now that really is a head scratcher. You're so tiny it makes foreplay hard. I could try to caress your boobs and end up fracturing a rib. I'd lick you, but I don't know where you've been. And erotic biting … not so much."

"Not trying to criticize here, but this plan doesn't make much sense. What are you gonna do, have me sit on your finger until I give in and call you Mist … that name? Cause I'm stubborn and I'm not gonna." My legs weren't feeling as confident as my mouth was; they were spread pretty wide and could do with a little break. Lauren didn't need to know that.

"I'm going to get you just to the edge of cumming. I'll give you the chance to call out my true title. And you better say it like you mean it. If you don't I'll stop everything and wait until you've cooled down enough to start over again."

"So you're going to edge me until I give in? That's the plan? Get me so horny I can't think straight?"

"You look like you get led around by your clit a lot."

"I'm getting off."

I tried lifting my right leg up so I could swivel around and dismount, but my poor legs were spread way too wide. I'd have never been able to get on this thing if Lauren hadn't air lifted me onto it. Even then I was worried that she might have broke something. I tried pushing myself up with my arms so my legs would rise with me and meet in the middle, but Lauren tapped my shoulder with her pinky. As far as she was concerned she barely touched me, but it was more than enough to slam me back down onto the well used toy.

"Sit." Lauren barked the order like I was a cocker spaniel. "You aren't going anywhere until you obey. Call me Mistress Lauren and I'll let you make a nice cummy on my finger. Doesn't that sound wonderful?"

"It sounds like trying to be sarcastic while talking dirty doesn't work."

"So back to the problem at hand, getting you in the mood without maiming you or icking me out." Lauren rubbed her chin mock thoughtfully. "You're wrong, by the way."

"About anything in particular, or everything?" Two could play the sarcasm game.

"Probably both, but especially about them paying me. To train you. They're not."

"So you're a ..."

"... an unpaid intern."

"I was going to say 'perv,' but same diff."

"Ever since I found out about this place I've been fascinated by the idea that people would do this to themselves. That they'd spend a buttload of cash getting turned into little useless vermin like you. That's like one step below being into autoerotic asphyxiation and having a bad sense of balance.

"I'm writing a paper about you. Resizeds in general and you in particular. Stovent lets me play with one of their guinea pigs and all I have to do is Eliza Doolittle her into some pop singer's purse pet. I get to root around inside that teeny tiny little head of yours to figure out why you're so fucked up. And Stovent gets to save a few bucks, so win-win."

"I'm not like that. I mean, sure, I'm small, but I never eroticized this."

"Whatever you say."

"I'm serious. I only did this for Tina."

"If you were that dumb before they shrank you I'm surprised you're not just drooling on the table stupid right now."

"Can you just get me off this, Lauren. It's hard and my legs are starting to cramp up. They won't be too happy with you if I end up hurt."

"Lightbulb!" Lauren's face lit up.

"Lightbulb?" I don't think I wanted to know.

"Like a lightbulb went off inside my head. I know how to get you in the mood without having to take you to the Fischer-Price emergency room. Role playing. You look like the type who loves that shit. God knows Greta did."

"I'm straddling the bastard child of a mechanical bull and a Sybian and you want to role play? Screw that, I'm not playing."

"I guess I'll just have to tell you the story of how we first met."

"That just happened and it wasn't very sexy. I crawled out of my bra, saw you, pissed myself in terror. I don't know what turns you on, but that did nothing for me."

"No. Not the real story. The fantasy."

Lauren looked me deep in the eyes. It was way more intense than I thought it would be. Each of her eyes was bigger than my head and she stared at me like I was made of glass and she was a dragon. She started to speak.

"Once upon a time there was a pretty young school girl named Lauren. Lauren was very young and innocent and oh so pretty. Picture me, only in a sexy school girl outfit. And keep me twenty or this gets real weird real fast.

"Lauren's Dad had to leave town for the weekend and he needed to find someone to look after his little girl while he was away. He thought he found the perfect babysitter. Her name was Becky and she seemed so wise and mature to Lauren's Dad, but she'd fooled him by shoving her premature double d's in his face.

"Becky acted polite and sweet when Lauren's Dad was still there, but al that changed the second he walked out the door and poor Lauren was left alone with the wicked Becky."

I felt Lauren fumble around beneath my sex saddle then the vibrator came to life.

"That's the lowest setting." Lauren said, taking an aside from her story.

"Th... this is the lowest?" She had to be lying. I'd used this toy over a hundred times and the low setting never felt like this. It was already going faster than a washing machine on spin cycle.

"I can turn it up if it's not enough for you."

"NO!"

I had to keep myself from getting excited. OK, too excited. I can get pretty stupid when I get horny. McCaskill showed me that. I was already in a hole with Lauren and I needed to show her that I could set boundaries, not give up even more of my control and dignity to her.

While I was fighting my inner demons, Lauren got back to her story.

"'What do we do now, Becky'? sweet Lauren asked.

"'Don't call me that'. the wicked Becky replied. 'You are to call me Miss Hogarth. And you better do everything that I tell you to do or you'll be sorry.'

"'Yes, Miss Hogarth. May I watch some television, Miss Hogarth'?" young Lauren asked.

"'Whatever! Just don't bother me or you'll be sorry'.

"Lauren turned on the television and flipped the channel to her favorite show. Only the show was too loud or maybe Miss Hogarth didn't like it. Sweet innocent Lauren didn't know. All she knew was that Miss Hogarth got real angry and yelled at her to change the channel.

"'I'm sorry, Becky. I'll turn it down. Just please let me watch my show'. Lauren begged.

"Before Lauren could blink, the evil Miss Hogarth jumped from the couch and slapped the young girl hard across the face, knocking her to her knees.

"'You didn't do what I told you. You didn't call me the name you were supposed to call me. And now you're sorry'. Miss Hogarth said, looking down at the frightened girl."

Lauren must have flipped another switch because the vibrations got even more intense. I could feel my body reacting to the powerful throbbing between my legs while my brain kept trying to picture Lauren dressed as a slutty Catholic school girl. Neither was helping.

"You're really bouncing around down there, aren't you?" Lauren said in her normal voice. As she had acted out her fantasy she gave her fantasy counterpart a Disney princess voice. Fantasy Becky sounded like a wicked stepsister. "Let me know if you need any help staying in the saddle."

I tried to tell her to go fuck herself, but words were hard.

"'Why are you so mean.' little Lauren called out from the floor. 'I'm going to call my Dad and he'll make you stop being mean to me.'

"But when little Lauren reached for her phone to call her Dad the wicked Miss Hogarth grabbed her arm and pressed it hard into her back and twisted it until Lauren cried. Miss Hogarth pushed little Lauren into the kitchen forcing her to crawl on her knees while the older girl kept her arm pressed tight against her back.

"Miss Hogarth pushed her into the kitchen, then across the kitchen floor, right up to the refrigerator. She reached into the refrigerator and pulled out one of Lauren's Dad's beers.

"Lauren knew she wasn't ever supposed to touch them, but the mean Miss Hogarth grabbed two. The sadistic babysitter opened both. She drank one and poured the other one down the front of Lauren's school blouse."

I was trying not to think of fantasy Lauren in a wet white blouse when real Lauren turned up the speed again. I tried to think about anything else other than the orgasm train coming in the distance, but that wasn't happening. Pretty soon I'd have to either stick to my guns and get blue beaned or say goodbye to my dignity and cum like a banshee.

"'Go on tell your Dad I slapped you.' wicked Miss Hogarth said. "I'll tell him that I caught you drinking his beer and that's why your face and your butt are so red.'

"'But my butt's not red.' little Lauren said from the floor. Tears were already starting to form in her perfect eyes.

"'I can take care of that.' Miss Hogarth pulled little Lauren off the ground and pushed her over her knee.

"Little Lauren began to kick her legs up and down, but she was so much smaller and weaker than Miss Hogarth that it didn't matter. She was helpless on Miss Hogarth's lap as the babysitter lifted up the pretty girl's short skirt. Lauren felt the older woman's hand glide up her defenseless legs, over her panties, and come to rest on her lower back."

Shut up. Shut up. Shut up. I screamed inside my skull.

"Lauren could feel Miss Hogarth put her fingers under the waistband of her panties. The young girl held her breath not believing that this was happening. She hadn't done anything wrong, but she was about to be punished like a little kid. The older girl was teasing her, torturing her, with the humiliating thought of being spanked bare assed naked in her own home."

The vibration between my legs was getting too intense. My body was doing things my brain couldn't stop. Besides, it was too busy deciding if I identified with Lauren or Miss Hogarth in this scenario. I could feel my climax building deep inside of me as Lauren continued to mouth out her role play.

"Miss Hogarth slowly lowered Lauren's white panties down to her knees and left them dangling there. The older girl placed her cold hand on the younger girl's warm butt and began to gently rub the tender flesh.

"Little Lauren lay there embarrassed and confused. Here she was, naked from the waist down on another girl's lap about to be spanked only Miss Hogarth wasn't spanking her. In fact it felt a little good.

"Then Miss Hogarth lifted her hand high in the air and brought it down hard on Lauren's defenseless backside. The slap of flesh on flesh sounded like thunder to the young girl. She yipped at the searing pain. She thought she was prepared for the second one, but that hurt worse than the first.

"By the third spank Lauren was crying. Her butt was on fire and she felt so useless and embarrassed. After the fifth she was flailing her arms and legs trying to get away from the older, larger girl. But Miss Hogarth used her other arm to pin Lauren's arms down and her flailing legs only kicked air.

"Lauren lost count of how many times Miss Hogarth's powerful hand rained down on her vulnerable backside. She'd stopped kicking and fighting somewhere after the fifteenth. By the time Miss Hogarth was done there was no fight left in Lauren. She lay there in agony until Miss Hogarth stood up.

"The defeated girl wanted to fall to the floor. It would be easier just laying there, crying, and feeling sorry for herself, but the older girl had other ideas. She pulled Lauren up to her feet.

"'I want you to stand in the corner, little girl.' Miss Hogarth said. 'Put your nose right up to the wall. Hold your skirt up. Don't pull up those panties. I want to see that blazing red butt of yours as I sit here and finish my beer and call my friends and tell them how stupid you are.'

"Lauren did as she was told even though she was totally humiliated. She stood there blushing while the older girl drank her Dad's beer and called her friends. She stood there and she thought about how things would change one day. How she would see to it that one day Miss Rebecca Hogarth was the small weak one. How she'd make the haughty bitch call her ..."

Lauren had given me the cue. This was it. I either said what she wanted to hear and this would be over with and I'd climax to my humiliation. Or I'd salvage my dignity for a little while longer. Cause that's all I could hope for, wasn't it? If she was willing to keep bringing me to the edge sooner or later I'd take the leap.

"BITCH!"

It wasn't the answer Lauren wanted, but it felt so good saying it.

Then the vibrations stopped and I was almost thrown from the vibe. Like being on a motorcycle that went from sixty to zero.

"no no no no. I was so close." I whined.

I ground my crotch into the hard plastic trying to push myself over the edge. I must have looked pathetic humping Lauren's sex toy finger, but I didn't care anymore. Now that the vibrator was turned off all I wanted to do was push myself over the edge. Without having to do what Lauren wanted me to do. OK, it was kinda childish, but I was having a really weird day so cut me some slack.

Lauren put her finger down on top of me, pinning my body down, stopping me from rubbing myself off.

"You are so close right now you'd probably cum in two minutes if I turn the vibe back on now. And I'll do it, if you do what I want. Now what do you call me?"

I closed my eyes and fought back the stupid horny begging me to call her Mistress.

"Lauren." I said, through gritted teeth.

"Stubborn little thing, aren't you? Let's see how everything's going in electric lady land."

Lauren placed her fore and middle fingers under my armpits and lifted me half way off the plastic vibrator. My aching legs rejoiced. I could see a wet streak glisten on the plastic where I'd sat. I was a little surprised it hadn't been a puddle.

Lauren ran her thumb past my butt and over my dripping labia. The feeling of contact and motion down there were good, but still not enough to get me off. I managed enough dignity and self control to not hump her thumb, but it wasn't easy.

"Somebody's happy to see me." Lauren ran her giant thumb back and forth over my desperate parts. "So hot. So wet. It's like a rainforest down there."

"Lauren, I'm not going to ..."

"Shh shh shhhhh." Lauren cooed down to me. She dropped me back down on the vibe and placed her thumb, still damp from my arousal against my lips. I'm ashamed to say I licked that thumb. My brain was just too oversexed not to taste myself.

"Whatever you were going to say doesn't matter. It's just your pride. Your body got shrunk so small, but your pride is still as big as a real person's. Just let go of that giant pride and you can feel so so good."

Lauren took her hand away from me. I hoped that she would turn the stimulator back on right away, but she just bucked her finger up and down taking me on a slow teasing ride to nowhere. It was just enough to keep me gagging for it, but not enough to push me over.

"Does it make it hotter for you, knowing that this isn't just a job for me? That I'm effing with your head for science and my own jollies?"

"Lauren, I am begging you. Please. Stop doing this to me. It's obvious I'm so much less than you. Why should it matter what I call you? Or if I get off on this stupid vibrator. Just leave me alone for a little while and I'll take care of myself. Or you can watch. At this point a little exhibitionism is almost normal. Just let me have this and we can get on with all the training you need me to do. Want me to literally jump through hoops, I'm your gal. Want me to play fetch with a gummi bear, I'm there. This means nothing to you, why can't you just let me have it."

"Because it means everything to you."

"I'm not **that** desperate. I can hold out." I didn't believe me either.

"I can literally do this all day. I have a drawer full of batteries and nothing better to do." Lauren said, continuing to slowly move me up and down. "So how'd you like my little fantasy?"

"You watched a lot of Cinemax."

"It's not that bad. You were about to cum your little brains out to it."

"I think the vibrator was doing the heavy lifting on that one, Lauren."

"Why don't we find out." Lauren said, launching back into her sex fantasy.

"Little Lauren remembered that day for the rest of her life. The humiliation of being stripped and spanked then forced to stand in the corner burned itself into her. The fact that her Dad believed Miss Hogarth and her tits over his own daughter only made it worse.

"Lauren grew up and learned everything she could about chemistry and biology. She wanted to make Miss Hogarth feel as powerless as she had felt. She Doogie Howsered her way through Master's degrees in both subjects and spent years perfecting her revenge until one day she created a pill that would make the older woman sorry.

"Lauren knew a bar that Miss Hogarth liked to go. She went there every night after work hoping to see Miss Hogarth and give the sadistic woman the revenge pill. After several nights of disappointment, Miss Hogarth finally walked into the bar. She was just like Lauren remembered her. A little older. A little rounder. But she looked at everybody like they were there to serve her or get out of her way. Lauren watched the older woman take a seat at the bar; all she had to do now was wait for the opportunity to drop the pill in Miss Hogarth's drink."

Lauren must have decided that I'd cooled down enough not to instantly pop if she hit the switch. I felt the compact engine whirr to life between my cramped legs. The supposedly lowest setting. Lauren stopped bucking me up and down leaving the vibrator and her Penthouse Forum fantasy to get me off.

"Miss Hogarth was on her second drink when Lauren took her chance. The former babysitter was busy talking to someone on the other end of the bar and wasn't looking too carefully at her drink. Lauren walked up and pretended to reach for the peanuts when she was really dropping her revenge into Miss Hogarth's drink.

"The little blue pill sizzled when it went into the alcohol. Lauren was worried Miss Hogarth might notice, but Hogarth was too wrapped up in herself to notice anything or anyone else. She certainly didn't notice her one time charge walking back to her table and watching to see what happened.

"It didn't take long for the pill to start taking effect. Not that Miss Hogarth noticed what was really happening. No, Miss Hogarth was feeling too dizzy and lightheaded to notice that she was getting just a little bit smaller. She'd shrunk by more than an inch by the time she decided to call it a night. Her clothes felt loose when she stood up, but she thought it must have something to do with her new diet.

"Lauren made it outside before Miss Hogarth. She'd managed to park nearby so she was in her car by the time the slowly shrinking babysitter stumbled out of the bar.

"'Miss Rebecca Hogarth?' Lauren asked after driving up to the disheveled woman. 'I'm Lauren your Uber driver.'

"'I don't remember getting an Uber.' Miss Hogarth said, but didn't sound too certain. She had been drinking. And she didn't feel so good. Maybe she had and forgotten about it.

"'If you say so, Ma'am, but somebody called me and I'm here now.' Lauren said. 'And you look like you could use a ride.'

"'Yeah. Sure. Why not?' Miss Hogarth stumbled into the back seat and collapsed. She gave Lauren an address. Lauren didn't bother learning it; she wasn't taking Rebecca home. Not Rebecca's home, anyway."

Real world Lauren ran the tip of her finger down my spine and up

my side. The giant pad of her finger brushed against the side of my
boob. I thought she was worried about lethal foreplay. Not that I
needed anything else to make this any harder.

"Lauren looked at Rebecca in the rearview mirror. She could see
that the older woman had shrunk another inch. Her once tight club
clothes now hung loosely on her smaller body.

"Lauren hit the child safety locks to prevent Rebecca from
making a run for it and adjusted the rearview mirror to give her the
best angle to watch Rebecca diminish."

Lauren took the wandering finger off me. I hadn't realized how
much heat she was giving off until it was gone and I felt the cool air
on my bare skin. I heard a pause in the narrative before it picked up
again. Then Lauren's giant finger was back. This time gently pressing
into my right breast. The tip was slick with a thin layer of moisture
from where Lauren had probably licked it.

The tip of her finger dwarfed my breast.

"Lauren drove Rebecca back to Lauren's home. By the time they
made it there Rebecca had lost several inches and was almost the
perfect size for what was going to happen next.

"'Where are we?' Rebecca asked. She'd woken up in the backseat
and was feeling very confused and woozy from the revenge pill.

"'You're late.' Lauren said. 'We have to get you inside and
changed right away. There isn't any time to argue.'

"Rebecca didn't feel good enough to argue so she let Lauren pull
her from the backseat of the car. Lauren laughed when Rebecca stood
up and her panties just fell down and landed on her feet. The once
tight dress almost followed it, but Lauren grabbed a hold of it before
it puddled on the floor at Rebecca's feet. Lauren directed the stunned
and shrinking woman forward, stepping out of her fallen undies and
into Lauren's home."

Lauren ran her wet finger from my breast to my arm and then up
my neck. I had to turn my head the other way to give the giant finger
room. I could feel my own twitching pulse echo back from the gentle,
but constant pressure.

"Lauren brought Rebecca into the kitchen. Rebecca was already
much smaller than Lauren and getting tinier by the minute. Lauren
had everything she needed on the table.

"'You have to get changed.' Lauren said. 'Quickly. If you're late
they'll punish you.'

"Lauren pulled the dress over Rebecca's head leaving the

shrinking woman in nothing but an oversized bra that was already falling off. Rebecca reached up to clutch that last piece of clothing to her much smaller chest, but Lauren slapped her fingers away, unhooked the bra, and tossed it in the sink with the dress.

"Rebecca covered herself with her hands while Lauren prepared her for her final revenge. Lauren made Rebecca step into a pair of plain cotton underwear. The sort that schoolgirls wore. In fact they were a girls size. Becky would never fit into her big girl panties again.

"The bra Lauren thrust into Becky's hands was equally juvenile, but the shrinking woman was glad to have anything covering her. She was still trying to think straight, but Lauren seemed so earnest she just had to obey."

Lauren moved her finger from the side of my neck to the back. The gentle pressure increased until I was forced forward and kept on going until I was laying flat on the giant sex toy. My breasts didn't know if they were aroused or in agony. The nipple that McCaskill had clawed felt like it was going to fall off.

"Lauren pushed Becky into a chair and rolled a pair of white knee high socks up her small, but still shapely legs. The white blouse came next. Lauren put it over Becky's head and helped her put her arms through the sleeves. It fit perfectly; Becky was the perfect size.

"Lauren stood Becky back up. The older woman barely came up to her chest now. Lauren handed the reeling girl a plaid skirt and the humbled girl pulled it on. The matching blazer completed the outfit.

"'Do you know what you're wearing, little Becky?' Lauren asked.

"Becky just shook her head too scared and confused to even open her mouth.

"'That's the exact same outfit I was wearing when you dumped beer on me and put me over your knee. Do you remember who I am?'

"'Lauren.'

"Lauren slapped Becky's face the second the name crossed her mouth. Little Becky tumbled to the floor on the verge of tears.

"'Call me Mistress Lauren or you'll be sorry.' Lauren had waited years to say those words."

I was so close.

The room got darker. No, not the room. Just the tiny part of it that I was occupying. Lauren must have leaned forward over me. I could see her long black hair falling around her hand like old growth rain-forest cutting out the light from the giant's portion of the room. I could feel her warm breath on my cold back.

I knew this was my cue, but I bit my tongue. I expected the story to end and the vibe to turn off, Lauren kept on going.

"But bad little Becky didn't obey. She just stood there dumbly so Lauren pulled her across her lap. She gave Becky time to kick her legs and try to escape. Just long enough for the terrified girl to know that now she was the helpless one.

"Then Lauren pulled up Becky's little schoolgirl skirt. She ran her fingers from the top of Becky's knee high socks to the waistband of her underwear. Just as the older woman had done to her all those years ago.

"Lauren took her time pulling down Becky's panties then she rubbed the scared woman's exposed butt, just as Becky had done to her."

I felt Lauren's finger run up my leg and come to rest on my own butt. Pushed forward like this I was half sitting, half laying on the stimulator. Her finger was on the part of my butt not touching the pink plastic.

Was she going to spank me like the Becky in her fantasy? That sort of thing led to internal bleeding for someone my size. She couldn't mean it.

The room grew darker as Lauren lowered herself even further and the only light getting to me was the little bit that made it through her giant hair. I felt something warm and wet and as big as I was press itself against my back and move up.

Lauren had just licked me.

"Call me by my true title or you'll be sorry." Lauren's face was so close to me I could hear her words inside my head. Her warm breath felt good against the trail of spit she'd made on my back.

I didn't know if she was talking to me or fantasy Becky or both.

The vibrator turned off.

I want to say that I handled the sudden lack of stimulation with grace and aplomb, but I really ended up grinding into it again for all I was worth.

Lauren's giant fingers lifted me completely off the stimulator and placed me on all fours on the table. I tried to stand up, but was pushed down by her impossibly strong fingers. Another finger reached under me and lifted me up by the tummy pushing my ass out and into the air. My toes weren't even touching the ground, my whole weight was being supported by Lauren's one finger with the little bit of balance my hands supplied.

"You aren't taking the carrot, so I'm bringing in the stick." Lauren said, her face still so close to my body I could feel her breath. "I'm going to be a nice goddess and give you a choice. Get off or get hurt."

Lauren underscored her point by running her giant tongue between my legs. I can't begin to describe what that felt like. To be invaded by something so familiar yet so alien. I'd had plenty of tongues swab my deck, but this was so completely different. It felt like a sea lion was trying to mount me. Only it was a woman. But not all of her.

I was still trying to do the mental gymnastics of that when I heard a loud flick followed by an immediate searing pain in my ass.

"Don't worry. I was sorta BS ing you about putting you in the hospital. I won't. You won't be sitting for a week once I'm done with you, but you'll be healthy otherwise. Now tell me what I want to hear and I'll give you your reward."

I didn't think I could stand another hit like that. Maybe she was right about knowing what she was doing, but I'm not sure many undergraduates really know what that means. And I was sooooo desperate for a good cum. Hell, even a shitty orgasm would relieve the pressure.

"So you're going to give me butt blistering pain or the most intense orgasm of my life?"

"I can't speak for the rest of the orgasms in your life, but it you say so, yeah. That's the deal in a nutshell."

I closed my eyes and put my head to the ground. I knew what I had to do, but that didn't make this any easier. I'd cave, but I didn't have to see that look of triumph in Lauren's eyes when I did.

"Then please let me cum, Mistress Lauren." I said as sweetly as I possibly could.

"No."

"Whaddya mean, 'no?'"

"'Whaddya mean, "no?"' Mistress Lauren." the bitch with my orgasm corrected me.

"You honestly expect me to keep on calling you that after you backed out on the deal?"

"Absolutely. When I was six my Mom promised me a pony if I cleaned my room. That didn't happen, but I still had to clean my room. I got over it, you will too."

"A pony is huge. I was promised one little mind blowing orgasm. Just now. The air you used to make the promise is still in your lungs."

"That's great, but I'm not hearing any 'Mistress Laurens.'"

"Screw you!"

"Look it's not like you haven't said it already. The thing you vowed to never ever say. Just call me it again and we can move on with your training."

"No way. And you can spank my butt till it glows purple, but I'm not gonna say it again."

"You're getting cranky."

"I am not. I am upset. There is a difference."

"I think someone needs a time out."

"Only if it's you and your lying mouth."

"It's my fault." Lauren said. "I got you overstimulated and now you're getting fussy."

"I'm so not fussy right now. But, yeah, I am overstimulated. And, yeah, it's your fault."

"That's it. You're in time out."

"What ya gonna do, make me stand in the corner of Barbie's dream home?"

"Don't be ridiculous; you are way too white trash for that neighborhood. Besides, you're way to small for Barbie's gig. I've got a much better place in mind."

"What? You gonna stick me down your pants."

"Actually ..."

"Do you not recognize sarcasm when you hear it? Or have you built up an immunity?"

"Come here, you."

" No, I will ..." I started to whine/protest, but Lauren's hand swooped down and snatched me up before I could explain my nuanced position vis a vis getting stuffed down her shorts.

I was starting to get used to being manhandled by giants. The unexpected speed of the Lauren behemoth was still a shock to me, but the experience wasn't making me want to hurl any more. If I could just get past the terrifying moments when I was hurtling through space clenched in a giant fist cage I could almost pretend I was going through a Star Trek transporter. Beaming from one part of the room to another.

I beamed down to the floor. The smooth tile felt cold against my bare feet making me do a little dance impossibly trying to keep my feet from touching.

I looked up and saw all of Lauren. Mostly I'd just seen her from the waist up since I was standing on a table. Yeah, I'd seen most of her walking away, but I was still elevated and she wasn't right on top of me. She'd already pulled down her pants with that disturbing giant speed. I couldn't even see her face from this close. My eyes traveled up bare legs that might as well have been two redwoods. Two soft and silky redwoods.

Did I mention how horny I was?

The sexy redwoods met in a canopy of beige underwear. I could see a couple square meters up her shirt, but nowhere near the fun parts.

"I appreciate the thong, but you really need to think about getting a Brazilian. Unless you're trying to replant the rainforest. In your pants."

"You take pills to stop periods. You don't like pubes. What's your problem with nature?"

"It doesn't get Netflix."

Lauren shock her head at my answer, pulled her thong down to her ankles and sat down around me. Literally. Her legs, bent at the knees with her feet flat on the ground were on either side of me tall as office buildings. My house-sized purse was tossed behind me. Lauren's vulva lay before me. I'm not sure, but I think it was taller than me.

"Uh, Lauren. I'd be lying if I said I hadn't read about this sort of thing on the net, but I really wanted Tina to be my first. And I'm not cool with using 'time out' as a euphemism for this."

"I'm not going to insert you." Lauren said. She was leaning down staring at her crotch and me so I could see her face again. "Gawd! All you vermin ever think about is getting stuffed up inside real people. Our mouths. Our vaginas. Our butts. Our noses."

"You're not stuffing me in your vajayjay?"

"You sound disappointed."

Maybe I was, but I wasn't going to give her the satisfaction of knowing. I was still feeling the heat of my recent ride on Lauren's sex saddle; at that moment just about anything sexual sounded like a great idea to me.

"I'm confused." I said, moving the topic away from my alleged disappointment. "If you're just gonna drop me down your pants, why flash me like this. I mean I appreciate a good show as much as the next gal, but what the eff, dude? Your lady junk is **right** there. Are you fishing for compliments?"

"I know what you're gonna do if I just stuff you down my drawers. Those restless hands are just going to end up between your legs and you're going to get off. I can't have that during time out. This is punishment, not play time. So I have to do something you're going to hate, but I'm bigger than you and I make the rules."

Lauren's giant arm reached over me and started rummaging around through my purse again. She pulled out a compact the size of an archery target, flipped it open, and placed it on the floor a few inches from her forested lips.

"This is going to be tricky. I'm not going to put up with any bullshit or whining from you. I need you to stand between me and the compact. I'll let you walk there yourself or I can put you there. You have two seconds to decide how it's gonna be."

I didn't know where this was going, but it didn't look like I had any good alternatives. I walked to the spot between the open compact and Lauren. I was more than a little intimidated standing in front of a super-sized vagina, close enough that I could just reach out and touch it. I swear to God I could smell the pheromones spreading out on the air.

I turned away from the living symbol of my inadequacy and looked in the small full length mirror. It was the first real good view I'd gotten of myself since I woke up in the Land of the Giants. My hair was a mess. I guess getting doused by the firehose faucet and letting it air dry wasn't the way to go. The necromancers must have washed the make up off of me before they cast their shrink spell. Either that or I shrank and the make up didn't and there's a pillow somewhere with my face on it.

My body looked the way I remember it looking. My nipples could cut glass, which wasn't normal, but understandable under the circumstances. I was covered in a thin sheen of sweat from my frustrating ride. I turned around and took a look at my butt. I could see a big red mark from Lauren's one hard spank. I rubbed it and gave Lauren the dirty look she deserved.

"I'm here; now what?" I called up. I was too close to see her face.

Lauren began to feel around her china like she was looking for something. I was about to tell her to stop beating around the bush, but my big mouth had already gotten me into enough trouble today. In a few seconds Lauren found what she was looking for, pulling a thick white rope from out of the hedge maze of her pubic hair.

"Why do you have a rope coming out of your who ha?" I asked.

"It's not a rope." Lauren said.

"Oh." I was confused. Then the penny dropped. "OH! You are NOT ..."

"Hush. I'm only going to use the string to tie your hands."

"To your tampon!"

"Yeah. It'll keep you from falling out or jilling off."

"It's like I'd be handcuffed to your tampon. Like one of those prison escape films only instead of a prison it's your thong and instead of a hardened jive talking con artist I'm handcuffed to your tampon and there isn't any escape cause the dogs are gonna catch our trail like THAT." and I snapped my little fingers.

"All you have to do is take your punishment like a woman and sit in there till I tell you it's over. Be a good thing and you'll never have to meet my Aunt Flo. Fuck with me, and I'll make you her bitch."

"What does that even mean?" I asked.

"You don't want to find out."

"But I hate my period."

"I know; I'm a good listener. And you talk a lot."

"That's not the point. Being handcuffed to a tampon that's in use is super freaking me out. It will be pure effing Hell for me in there."

"Kinda my point." Lauren didn't sound sympathetic. At all. "You should have done what I told you."

"I'm not very good at this, so please grade this on a curve." I dove to my knees facing the giant hairy vulva and raised my clenched hands to the sky. "Please Mistress Lauren. My goddess who art in Heaven, hallowed be thy name. You're right. I'm stupid and proud and vermin. I get that. Now. I should have done what you said, but I was still thinking like a real person. You are so much smarter and wiser than me. You know what's best. I see that now, Mistress Lauren. I'm a changed … thing. I will do everything that you tell me as soon as you tell me. Just please don't make me take a time out tied to your tampon."

"That was perfect." Lauren's voice boomed down from the Heavens.

"Thank you, Mistress Lauren. Thank you."

"Hold that position and close your eyes, vermin."

"Yes, Mistress Lauren. Thank you, Mistress Lauren."

I may have been laying it on thick, but inside I was still doing a happy dance celebrating my near brush with giant menstruation. As demeaning as it was to kowtow to Lauren, it beat the alternative.

Then I felt a loop of rope go over my raised hands and pull tight.

"I was good. I apologized." I screamed up at the dick god I'd been saddled with.

"And I'm sure there are a lot of people on Youtube who are going to just love that. Now stand still, I'm standing on my head doing this backwards in a mirror. One screw up and I cut off your circulation. Or pull out your very own cotton pony. You wouldn't like that."

"This is so unfair."

I was close to tears. In my head I had this idea of what being Tina's dolly would be like. It was cute and sexy and sweet. Not this. This was just one person being mean to another because they could get away with it. And now that I was knee high to Skipper everyone could get away with it.

"Get ready for take off." Lauren announced when she was finished tying me up.

Lauren stood up suddenly pulling me off my feet and into the air. I was terrified that the force would wrench my shoulders, but it wasn't that bad. I weighed less than a kitten so I guess that made sense. I dangled between Lauren's legs moving back and forth bouncing back and forth between her pubic mound and thigh gap. I tried to pull my-self up with the rope then remembered what it was attached to. I might not weigh much, but I might be able to pull hard enough to recreate the prom scene from Carrie.

Lauren pulled up her underwear and carefully positioned me inside. My face was planted right on the seam of her vulva on the closed outer lips. My body was cushioned in her soft, slightly scratchy pubic hair. The thong was snapped into place and I was held firm. I could see light out of the corner of my eye until Lauren pulled her pants up. It was just me, her pussy, and our tampon alone in the dark.

"I always wondered what it would be like to have a dick." Lauren's voice came down from the world outside her pants.

"erry unnee" Word to the wise; being pressed face first into a giant pussy is not good for your elocution.

"You're right, dick. You **are** very small. I better be sure the other boys don't see you in the locker room or they'll tell all the pretty girls I'm hung like an acorn."

I had my blistering put down ready, but I breathed in pubic hairs the moment I tried to release my brilliant bon mots.

"Whatever you did just then. That felt nice. Keep that up and I might pack you more often."

My revenge would be a dish best served cold. For now I'd have to get through this.

"This" was a mixed bag.

I like to think the tampon and I had an understanding. It stayed on its side of the labia and I stayed on mine. That didn't stop me from thinking about what it was doing over there and more than mildly freaking out about it.

At least I had other things to take my mind off that. And by other things I mostly mean sex.

I don't want to sound like some kind of perv who obsesses over sex like an internet troll on Xhamster. I can go for huge stretches of time without even thinking about doing anything with my junk or anybody else's. But I think any normal person would be laser focused on what was going on between their legs if they'd been through what I'd been through in the last twenty minutes. This may be TMI, but I was gushing. Like a fountain. But my hands were tied and the soft hair I was face planted into made it impossible to rub one out by rubbing on Lauren (don't judge me, you weren't there.) There was nothing I could do about it other than breathe in more of Lauren's pheromones and get more and more frustrated,

And then there was the heat.

Underwear wasn't meant to be worn by more than one person at a time. Most underwear, anyway. I was laid out on a warm blanket of tufty hair and being worn under panties as thick as a circus tent under jeans thicker than the tarp they cover baseball fields during rain delays. Two minutes after the jeans went up and the lights went out I was sweating like a Swede in the sauna. Naturally a lump of hot girl flesh down her pants got Lauren's genitals sweating too. The perfect storm for a truly miserable wet heat.

I'm not sure exactly what Lauren was doing in the world outside her pants. I could tell that she was standing and guess that she was walking around every once in awhile. Maybe she was playing on her phone. Maybe she was doing some light filing. She could have been juggling for all I knew. That's just it, I had no way of knowing. Which sucked on toast. I'm not going to say that forced ignorance was the worst part of being this helpless; it just wasn't something I'd thought about when I fantasized about my new life with Tina.

I started to count out the seconds. I needed something to do and knowing how long I'd endured being trapped in Lauren's underwear. But I kept getting distracted and lost count. The heat and the dark weren't helping either. I'd start counting and then feel myself napping off. Then Lauren would take a step or shift her leg and the fleshquake would snap me to consciousness.

I struggled for a long time and finally managed to turn my face away from Lauren.

"How long am I in time out?" I asked. It felt so good to be able to talk again.

"Do you have a watch?" Lauren asked.

"No." I tried to milk all the snark I could out of the one syllable.

"That's ok. I'll let you know when you can come out."

I started my brilliant response, but Lauren adjusted herself and me until my face was once more planted firmly against her sweaty flesh. I fumed inwardly and kicked Lauren as hard as I could, which wasn't very since I could barely move my foot.

I returned to my semi-waking purgatory and tried to force myself to sleep. I heard a giant door open followed by a familiar voice.

It was Tina.

Five: Visiting Days

"Hi, I'm looking for Lauren."

Tina! It was Tina. I could tell that even through Lauren's pants.

"You found her." Lauren shifted her position when she spoke.

What was Tina doing here? Wasn't there something somewhere about not seeing me until the big day? Or was that just brides?

"I'm Rebecca's new owner to be. Tina Jordan. I was hoping to see her before I left."

no no no no no no no no no

"I didn't think you were able to make it."

"That was a little white lie. My lawyer thought it best I didn't meet Rebecca till after she got ..."

"...small."

"Yeah." Tina said, she sounded a little embarrassed to be talking about my size. "So. Can I see her?"

Tell her no, I mouthed into Lauren's lady junk. Tell her no, Mistress Lauren. I added the Mistress part just in case Lauren's pussy could read my lips. I wasn't super rational at the time.

"She's in a time out."

Yes! I'm being punished. I can't see anybody.

"Time out?" Tina asked.

"She's been super naughty."

No need to go into details, Lauren. Keep it simple.

"Already?"

"Yeah, I tried being super nice to her to get her to do what I told her to do. You know, for her safety training. I even let her play with her favorite toy. But she didn't want to follow instructions so I had to put her in a time out."

LIES!

"That sounds like a baby punishment." Tina said.

"It's the only way she'll learn. She may look like a tiny adult, but her brain is barely at the toddler level. That's just science."

It is not!

"Can I still see her? Just for a minute. It's just that I don't have much time and I won't be able to get back here until her graduation."

Please. If you do one nice thing for me in your entire lifetime, Lauren, please don't let her see me like this.

"The thing is, right now, she's in my pants."

"In your jeans?" Tina asked.

"It's gonna sound weird, but underwear."

"You have Rebecca in your underwear?"

"Science says it's the only way."

"Could you … pull her out for a minute?" Tina's voice had a slightly grossed out edge to it.

No! On so many levels, no.

"Not without an accident. The kind you write letters to Seventeen about."

"I have no idea what you mean."

"It's best I don't explain it." Lauren said.

"Can I see her anyway?"

"Like, take a peek down my panties?"

"Yeah."

"That's kinda weird."

"So's keeping my pet in your undies."

"Touche."

"I'll pay you a 1,000 dollars if you let me."

"OK."

shitfuckshitshitfuck

Lauren dropped her jeans like a bad habit. The tight underwear that had held me imprisoned for so long got pulled away. I felt the flesh under me shift as Lauren contorted herself to give Tina the best possible angle on my humiliation. I slowly, and wetly, slid to the bottom of the pulled back underwear. I wanted to curl up in the fetal position, but my hands were still tied to Lauren's vagina with the tampon string. It forced my hands upward in their double prayer fist.

Bright light and cold air flooded in. After all that time in the dark the sudden reintroduction to light was blinding me. Looking upwards at it was too much form me even with my eyes closed. So I turned my head away and waited for this to be over.

Tina was about to see the little freak in another girl's panties. There was no way she could ever love me after seeing what a pathetic mess I was.

A little piece of my soul shriveled up and died when I heard Tina cry out —

"Oh my GAWD!"

I didn't dare open my eyes. I didn't dare look up. The woman I loved was up there staring down at me and I couldn't stand to see the look of disgust on her face. There was no way she'd want me after seeing me like this. I felt like shit. I looked like shit. I was confused and sweaty and literally chained to another woman's junk. I wasn't going to be with Tina; I was going to the Island of Misfit toys.

I felt the tears rolling down my face before I realized I had cried them.

"You are soooo cute." Tina cooed down to me.

I stopped mid-sniffle and tried to wrap those words around my little head. She couldn't mean it. She must have been teasing me. Trying to get my hopes up only to shove all my mistakes back in my face. I didn't think Tina was that mean. I must have done something to deserve it.

"Is she OK?" Tina asked Lauren.

"It's probably just a little overwhelmed. To it we're big and scary. This one peed down her leg when she first saw me. Give her a little bit and she won't stop talking. Literally."

"It's all right, little Becky. Tina's here now and you don't need to be scared anymore. No one's going to hurt you or make you feel bad. If they try they'll have to answer to me."

The ground beneath me shifted as Lauren adjusted her position. The tip of a giant finger rested on my chin and gently turned my head upwards until I was staring into Tina's beaming face.

"God, you're pretty." I said more out loud than I'd planned.

"And I could just eat you up." Lauren moved her finger down to my exposed belly and tickled me until I smiled.

"That's a thing, actually." Lauren said, while Tina was cheering me up. "Technically you can do anything you want with it once you bring it home, but Stovent's big on plausible deniability ixnay on the voreay."

"Shut up, Lauren. Tina's saying nice things about me."

"Hey, that wasn't very nice, Rebecca. Lauren's only doing her job. There's no reason to be rude about it."

"I'm sorry."

Please don't be mad at me. Oh please, oh please. Go back to making me smile. I'm positive you were about to call me pretty.

"Don't apologize to me; apologize to Lauren."

"I'm sorry, Lauren." That Tina heard me.

"That didn't sound very sincere." Tina chided.

"And it forgot something." Lauren added.

"What?" Tina asked.

"She knows."

Why couldn't you just stay out of this, Lauren. This would have been perfect if it weren't for you.

"We're waiting, Beck Beck."

Tina Jordan called me Beck Beck.

"I'm sorry, Mistress Lauren. What I said was very rude of me. I know that you're just trying to do what's best for me. It's just hard for me to understand that some times." I did the closest approximation to a curtsy I could manage standing on the gusset of another woman's under pants with my hands shackled to her hoo ha.

"That was totes adorbs, Becks."

"Thank you, Mistress Tina." I bowed my head as I basked in the praise.

"I'm not really a 'Mistress' type."

"I could call you Goddess." I'd already thought of her that way. Even before I fell down the rabbit hole.

"Just call me 'Tina' for now. Maybe we can figure something out later. Right now I really need to catch my plane if the Atlanta concert is going to start on time. I'll see you again when you're all trained and ready to come home with me. While I'm gone I want you to be a good girl for your Mistress Lauren. I'm giving her my personal number. If you get rude or naughty again I'll know. Do you promise to be a good girl?"

"I promise."

"And that Lauren won't have to call me?"

"She won't."

"That's my good girl." Lauren kissed the tip of her finger and pressed that kiss onto my cheek.

Lauren shifted back into a more comfortable position and Tina's face disappeared from view. I felt a little colder. Like the sun had set. Then Lauren snapped her panties back into position and pulled her jeans up and my world was sweaty and dark again.

Only instead of being totally miserable I was dancing on clouds. Tina was everything I knew she would be. And more. Our lives together are going to be fantastic. And she thought I was cute and adorable and probably pretty. My doubts and second guesses vanished.

I waited for the sound of the door, but heard Tina say something in a language I didn't understand. So not English. Probably Japanese. Her Mom was from there so that made sense.

Then I heard Lauren reply.

Lauren could speak Japanese? Should I have learned Japanese? Will I have to? If Tina asked me to I would; I'd do anything for my Goddess.

I nestled in to my punishment and dreamed about what life would be like being owned by a woman like Tina.

I ran like fuck; hard and not that well.

For one thing, I was never the sort of person who just ran just for the fun of it. If I needed to get someplace there was always a convenient internal combustion engine to get me there. Running was for getting away from monsters and getting to little kids with their hands down the garbage disposal and there haven't been many of either in my life.

So I was out of practice.

Then there was the boob issue. Mistress Lauren wouldn't give me any clothes. Not even a sports bra. So I was either running with my hands going up and down like a normal person while my boobs pretended the rest of my chest was a bouncy house or I held them in my hands. If you've never tried doing that, it's pretty damn awkward and slows you down.

My route to the diving board was blocked by a metric shit ton of obstacles that I was supposed to navigate. Lauren blah blah blahed about how this was simulating a real world survival situation, but really I just think she's got on hell of a sadistic streak.

Most of what I was climbing, jumping, and running around were kids' toys. Legos. Dolls. Lincoln logs. Yeah. I was surprised they still made those too.

Mixed in with the toys were items from my purse thrown about randomly. I'd manage to climb over Raggedy Andy's leg to come face to face with my drivers license blown up to the size of a poster. The sad thing was I probably looked better in that picture than I did running through Lauren's course. So far I'd had to get around my anti-period pills, my wallet, a Portuguese-English phrase book. The receipt for the last normal dress I was ever going to own, and a three month old fortune cookie.

I had made it around the crayon box and could just see the diving board ahead. It wasn't a real diving board of course. When you're this small nothing that looks normal is real. No, my diving board was one of those cheap flat wooden paint stirrers. It was glued to the side of the sink by a thick coat of green paint that had been allowed to dry there.

This was my fourth time through Lauren's obstacle course since she untied me from her … you know and took me out of her panties. I had made it to the diving board twice, but I missed the ring each time and ended up falling onto the dress they had lined the sink with to cushion my failure. It was my dress. The one I still had the receipt for. The one I was supposed to show off to Tina before it wouldn't fit me anymore.

Did I mention that Lauren is a dick?

I was sweaty and breathing hard. I felt drained. But Tina had told me to be a good girl for Lauren. It wasn't going to be easy. Remember, Lauren's a dick. But I was going to make Tina proud of me or die trying. After three failures I was leaning towards the latter.

I made my way to the diving board and focused on the ring. It was a good sized hoop dangling on a line. I tried not to think about what it really was – one of Lauren's oversized retro earrings, or that it was dangling on a line attached to a fishing pole the size of a red-wood. I didn't need to think about that. I just needed to know that it was a ring on a line and it was the safe way to the final part of the course.

I stopped and put my hands on my knees. I bent forward and took in several deep breaths. I was dying inside and needed a break before I tried to make the jump.

I didn't hear Lauren move up to me, but I felt the warm stream of vinegar water spray me from behind. I hated it. Every time I'd stop or catch my breath Lauren would swoop down with a spray bottle filled with warm vinegar water and spray me like you'd do a cat who was trying to get into mischief with her favorite sofa.

"Bad rat! No stop!" Lauren called down to me.

"Yes, Mistress Lauren." I said out loud. In my head it came out 'Fuck you, Cunty McDickface.'

I started running at the diving board. My bare feet crunched the dry paint before making it onto bare wood. I looked at my target and I timed my jump. I was bounced through the air by a combination of overtired leg muscles and the spring of the wood. I flailed my hands forward hoping to finally make contact with the ring and not collapse in failure into my own dress.

I felt something metal hit my hand hard. My wrist felt like it was about to explode. My first instinct was to pull it towards me to keep it away from the pain, but I forced it to grab hold of the ring.

And I did.

I didn't weigh much, but it was enough to lower me down to the center of the sink. I may have felt like total crap, but I also felt amazing. This must be how Batman feels every day.

I made it down to the sink level and let go of the ring. There was just one more thing to do and I would have beat Lauren's course.

The rat trap.

It was a humane trap. The ones with glue on them to keep the rat from running away or biting you. In the middle of the glue was a giant red button that Lauren had stuck there. It was plastic and fake, but I had to make it there and push it to win.

The only problem was, it was too far to jump and I'd get stuck halfway there if I tried to walk. I still had the line. I might be able to swing myself over there and jump. Then I remembered how my first two tries at the ring had gone. Or the disaster in my bra. I really didn't want to face plant into industrial strength glue.

Maybe I could do something with the dress. It formed a ring around the sink with the trap sitting in the middle of clear space. If I could just pull the dress a few inches I'd be able to cover the glue and walk to the button. And ruin my old dress.

I saw Lauren out of the corner of my eye aim the spray bottle at me and hauled butt before she gave me another humiliating spray. Jeez Louise, can't a gal have a moment to think?

I grabbed ahold of the dress with both hands and gave it a hard pull. Nothing.

I tried again this time pushing back with my feet as well. More nothing.

"The square cube law says I should be super strong now. How come I can't lift a damn dress?"

"Stovent found some exceptions to that law. Be grateful, if they hadn't you'd be dead right now." Lauren said. "Speaking of which, if this was real, you'd already be dead by now. Stop sucking so much."

The dress wasn't budging. That left me with the line, the earring, and the high likelihood that I'd end up hugging the glue trap.

Then I had the most brilliant idea ever. Only it turned out I was too weak to pull any of the buttons off the dress either.

It would have been perfect. I could have placed the dress buttons down to make little stepping stones to the big red win button. I would have won and I'd look cute doing so.

"Are you giving up or do I need to spray you again?" Lauren asked. She sounded bored.

"No. I'm doing it."

With nothing better to do and no real plan I grabbed the ring. Maybe I'd get lucky and make it on my first try. But that seemed about as likely as Kermit the Frog hosting the Tony's. It was a pretty big rat trap, but I only had to swing ten, maybe twelve, of my feet, but I wasn't exactly American Gladiators material.

I took a swing and flew over the glue. And right past the button. And onto the glue on the other side. I didn't so much face plant as lose my grip on the ring at the end of my arc and thud to the sticky ground on my butt.

"I hope you have some solvent for this, Mistress Lauren. If not, we're looking at the world's most painful Brazilian."

"You do realize that you're not getting out of here until you successfully complete this obstacle course in half the time it took you to fail this last time."

"What?!"

"That's right, no making kissy faces with Tina Jordan until you do this right."

"Yes, Mistress Lauren. Are you going to make me do it again?"

"I was going to let you go to bed, but if you'd rather embarrass yourself some more ..."

"No. Bed is good. I thank bed."

"Let me get the solvent and I'll get you ready."

Lauren carefully removed me from the trap and placed me on another table without the obstacle course set up. She unfolded a moist towelette and laid it out on the floor before me like a beach blanket.

"That's your shower for tonight. Get yourself clean while I get your night things together."

I looked at the wet towel and shrugged my shoulders. Of all the things I'd had to do today washing myself with it wasn't that bad. Sure a hot steamy shower would be great, but I was too pooped to argue. I just wanted to get to sleep and do better tomorrow.

" ... uh ... Mistress Lauren." I said as I began to rub the towel over my sore achey body. "I was wondering about where I was going to sleep tonight. I know I'm going to be a pet, but the word 'doll' has been thrown around a lot too. So am I going to stay in a pet cage? Like the vermin I am. Or ... maybe a custom fitted doll house with running water, electricity, and cable?"

"Neither. Tina has specific instructions about how she wants you to sleep with her. So we're going to be training you."

"Oh."

"Before you say anything else, do you have to make potty?"

"Mistress Lauren, I'm an adult woman. You don't have to talk to me like I'm a toddler."

"Does little Becky need to use the potty before night nights?"

On the one hand she was massively dissing me. On the other, she did just call me by my name for the first time ever.

"Actually I could … use a rest room." I said, trying to take the high road. "You're not gonna make me use a litter box are you?"

"No."

Lauren put a thimble down on the floor in front of me.

"Is that what I think it is, … Mistress Lauren?"

"That's your potty. Hurry up, I need to get you into your night night clothes."

Lauren just stared at me and my thimble potty waiting to see what I'd do next.

"You know, I think I'll just hold it till morning." Translation: I'll go pee in a corner when you're not looking.

"All right then. Let's get you dressed."

I felt giddy at the thought of getting my first set of doll clothes. I'm not exactly Ms Prude, but there's a feeling of vulnerability and weakness that comes from strutting around naked all the time. I felt that way enough just being the size I was, I don't need anything else to make me feel worse. Still, it was strange that my first outfit was going to be sleepwear.

"First we need to get you in your dolly diaper."

"My what?"

"Your dolly diaper. You won't be able to get up in the night to use the potty so you have to wear a dolly diaper."

"Is there another option?"

"No. Every night you'll be placed in your dolly diaper. If you're lucky you won't have to make potty and you'll have a dry night. If not, I'll take your dolly diaper off in the morning and let you clean yourself up."

"Can you call it something other than 'dolly diaper?' It sounds super creepy when you say it like that."

"No. Now lay on your back and I'll slide your dolly diaper up your legs."

I felt the mild pressure my bladder was exerting. There was no way I was going to be able to last the night. I either had to pee in a cup while Lauren watched or do it in the diaper overnight. Neither option was that great, but peeing in a thimble wasn't going to lead to diaper rash.

"I changed my mind about using the bathroom, Mistress Lauren."

"Do you mean the potty?"

"… yes."

"Then ask nicely. And call it what it is."

"May I … may I please use the potty, Mistress Lauren."

My cheeks were burning from the humiliation. Here I was, a full grown … an adult woman asking some girl if I could please use the potty before she put me in diapers for the night. I wasn't exactly the Queen of the World before I signed on to be shrunk down, but I'd never been this low until today. And this wasn't even the worse thing.

"Of course." Lauren said.

Lauren still made no attempt to look away or give me the slightest hint of human modesty. I stepped forward and gave it a gentle kick. It seemed sturdy enough. And the bottom was flattened enough so that it stayed upright. I didn't have any clothes to move out of the way so I just squatted down until my thighs rested on the edge of the cool metal.

I had my back turned to her, but I could feel Lauren's eyes staring through me as I was about to commit a very private act. My bladder was bursting to go, but my brain was sending too many mixed signals for it to void.

"I think little Becky is just looking for an excuse to stay up past her bed time." Lauren said.

"No, Mistress Lauren. I'm just a little pee shy. I'm not used to … any of this."

"I'll give you to the count of ten to start making night night potty. If you can't make by then you don't need to go and I'll get you dressed for bed.

She started her countdown.

I finally managed to force myself go by the time she reached "three." My face burned at the sound of my pee hitting the dented metal. I looked around for any sort of toilet paper. There wasn't any so I used the edge of my shower towel. Don't judge me, it was disposable and I needed something.

"Good. Now lets get you dressed in your dolly diaper and nighty." Lauren took the thimble away and gestured for me to lay down on my back.

The diaper turned out to be a cross between a regular disposable and a pair of pull ups. Lauren made me put my legs up and just glided them over my hips on over my butt.

"I could have pulled them up myself." I said.

"Yeah, but this way you remember who's in charge. Now stand up and let me take a look at you."

It took me a few extra seconds to get up with the massive bulk between my legs.

"How do they feel?" Lauren asked.

"Humiliating."

"I meant physically."

"I can't close my legs with all this … stuff in the way. And it's trapping all the heat in. I've been in these one minute and it's already feeling like there's a sauna in my shorts."

"How about the waistline? Too lose? Too tight?"

I put my hand flat on my hip and pushed my fingers down into the waistband. I was able to reach down and touch the bottom of the diaper.

"Goldilocks would love 'em; not too tight, not too loose." I said.

"I was worried about that. We can't have you putting your hands down your diapers like a naughty girl, now can we?"

"If I'm any part of that 'we,' then I am very much in favor of my hands going anywhere I want them to be."

Lauren ignored me and reached over my head for something out of my line of sight.I thought she was reaching for another diaper. A smaller sized one that would be even less comfortable than the one I was wearing. Then I heard the sound of something getting pulled and ripped. It almost sounded like sheet metal, but it turned out to giant piece of clear tape.

"Put your arms up in the air, Becky. Like a ballerina."

I didn't like where this was going, but sometimes playing ballerina was the better part of valor.

As soon as my arms were out of the way Lauren used her freakish giant speed to wrap the tape around my waist getting the sticky film half on the diaper, half on my skin. Taking this off was going to be a new level of Hell.

"Try putting your hands down your pants now."

My hand just slid on the smooth tape. Try as hard as I could, I couldn't even get my hand under the sticky side of the tape.

"I can't, Mistress Lauren."

"Sweet. Now let's get you in your nighty. Put your arms up up again. Like a pretty little ballerina."

"You really don't need all that extra coaxing. You can just ask me to raise my hands. Or, you know, let me put it on myself."

"Up up."

Clearly I was the only one who payed any attention to what I said.

"Yes, Mistress Lauren." and I obeyed.

I caught a brief glimpse of pink before I felt the dress being pulled over my head and down my body. Whatever it was it felt soft and smelled a lot better than I did. Lauren fastidiously adjusted every little bit of the dress before moving her giant hands back far enough for me to get a good look at the first outfit of my brave new world.

"This is actually pretty darn nice." I said, surveying my new threads. "I was half expecting some frou frou doll abomination, but this is pretty snazzy. Thank you, Mistress Lauren."

I gave a twirl and let the pink skirt float in the air. I ended with the best curtsy I could manage. You know, given the tape and the diaper.

It was more of a nightgown than a nighty with a flared skirt and these short pixie ball sleeves. It was made out of super soft cotton and it fit me perfectly.

"So here's the deal." Lauren said as I was admiring myself. "Tina has decided that she wants to sleep with you."

The happy stunned look on my face told Lauren exactly what was going on in my head.

"I'm not talking about sex. That's between you and her. I'm talking about sleep. 'Perchance to dream' and all that other stuff. She's decided that she wants to share her bed with you. And that's totally her call and cool, but we need to get you both ready for something like that."

"It's just sleep, Lauren. I've been doing that all my life."

"If Tina rolls over the wrong way you could suffocate under her and she wouldn't know you were dead until she woke up in the morning."

"That's a very good point, Mistress Lauren. Please tell me everything I need to know about not getting smooshed." I could be very polite and attentive when my life was on the line.

"We gave Tina a little electronic version of you."

"You gave Tina a robot me?!"

"More like a tamagotchi. It's about your size and can tell if something she did would have killed real you." Lauren said. "While she's learning that, you're going to be learning how to sleep with me."

"OK." I kept my voice as polite as I could, but Lauren was a few dozen steps down from Tina.

"Tina wants you to sleep on her chest. Near her heart."

"Oohhh." I put my hand to my own heart. Tina was so sweet.

"So that's where you'll be sleeping on me."

"But I don't love you."

"You're not a person, little Becky, but if you were a person you wouldn't be my favorite person either."

"But I'll roll off." your flat boyish chest. Inner me was still allowed to be catty, even if outer me had to be a good girl.

"We got you covered. I've got a special sleep bra with a pet compartment in-between my boobs. I practiced with my own Becky tamagotchi after we knew you were coming."

"And e-me survived?"

"Most of the time."

I woke before the alarm. Again. I'd been doing that a lot lately.

No, this isn't me waking up after my first night of sleeping between Lauren's boobs. I'd have to have gotten some sleep in order to wake up. And I got none that night. Trying to sleep on ground that's breathing is freaky as fuck.

I'm fast forwarding through the next few weeks. My first day as a shrunken person trainee was pretty much the same as the rest of my time at Stovent. Up to this morning. This morning was different. But the rest of the time it was just Lauren being mean to me and me being all brilliant and sassy. At least as much as I could get away with.

I was getting the hang of being so small.

I still wasn't allowed clothes during the day. I'm sure there are a lot of you out there who happy to hear that. You're called pervs. But I did wear a nightgown to bed each night. Tina got me seven nighties in all the colors of the rainbow. Even indigo, which I had always thought was just that guy from Princess Bride.

I also spent each night in what I'm going to call my protective underwear cause calling it a dolly … you know, makes it sound like I'm in a bad fairy tale or a good horror movie. For all you pervs at home, no, I did not have any overnight accidents. Though Lauren did wake up to me doing a potty dance in her bra. It's not as sexy as it sounds.

Lauren was with me almost all the time which I thought was weird. I got the impression that there was supposed to be a whole team of people training and caring for me not just one sarcastic intern.

Speaking of which; whoever set up that internship must have really hated Lauren. Which I can totally understand.

So I did pretty much whatever Lauren did. Lauren went to bed, I'd go to bed. Lauren had lunch, I'd eat some crumbs from her sandwich. Lauren needed to be mean, I got to run drills through the obstacle course. Lauren asked me a lot of questions about what I was going through. She really seemed to want to get inside my head. And I'm not sure that it was all for her paper either. I think a part of her really really got off on having that much power over someone else. And hearing me tell her about how weak and degraded I felt just made her hotter.

The only time I really had to myself was lap time. That was the hour or two between the end of the last training exercises and bed time. Lauren watched her TV shows on her phone while I laid on her lap doing nothing. She used ear buds so I couldn't even hear what she was watching. I tried talking to her, but she spray bottled me until I shut up. Everything else she'd done to me had been demoralizing and dehumanizing. Laying there on her lap with nothing to do really made me feel like a pet. Especially when Lauren lightly scratched my neck or petted me.

And my feelings towards Lauren were getting complicated. No, I wasn't falling in love with her. There isn't enough Stockholm Syndrome in the world for that to happen. But things were getting weird between us. Lauren kept going back and forth from being and ok kind of gal to being a total douchebag to me. My time out was probably the worst thing she did to me, but there were other things. Like tossing me in her filthy sock one time and hanging me up like a bag of laundry. She didn't let me out until the sock had gone from soaking wet with her sweat to crunchy.

Oh yeah, my arms were taped to my sides so I couldn't jill off. Like I was going to rub one out while breathing in her stinky feet. I don't know why Lauren was so obsessed with me being orgasm free, but she made sure that I never got off. If she so much as thought I was trying any happy business she'd spray me with that damn spray bottle until I put my hands "up up" and far away from my desperate lady junk.

So I was kinda obsessed with sex and living 24/7 with a woman who thought getting me all hot and bothered was funny as hell. The worst were the nights when she masturbated. If I spent an extra few seconds wiping myself I got the spray bottle, but Lauren was able to go to Funkytown anytime she wanted to. You know what Hell feels like? Hell is being the horniest person on the planet, getting strapped down onto a woman the size of an air craft carrier, right in-between her giant breasts, and getting to feel every breath she takes, every move she makes as she brings herself off to the orgasm that you so desperately need.

Then there's the shower.

By that point I'd gotten used to Lauren seeing me running around naked. She saw me do **everything.** After awhile you just get used to that. I don't even think Lauren was gay so it wasn't like she was getting off to seeing my boobs bounce around. She got off on the power trip in spite of my plumbing. But I never saw that much of Lauren. She dressed conservative on a budget – jeans, sneakers, t-shirts. Nothing that flashy or sexy.

But in the shower I saw everything. And I felt so damn guilty about it.

Showering with a normal person was intense enough on its own. Showering with a giant? Off the scale. You know those built in plastic shelves they have in some showers? The ones that are built into the siding, that you're supposed to put bath gel or shaving cream on? Lauren put a strip of ribbed and waterproof contact paper on one of those so I could stand on it without taking a high dive to the bottom of the tub. There was a sliver of soap and an upside down bottle cap with some shampoo in it there for me to use. At least I didn't have to shave. The necromancers must have done something to me when they shrank me; my pits and legs were still smooth weeks after I last ran a razor over them. Standing there I'd get a little bit of the spray from the shower, but most of the water that came my way bounced off of Lauren's giant naked body.

That's when things start getting complicated inside my head. I was already as horny as a fifteen year old boy at a strip club. I didn't want to have sexy thoughts about Lauren. I'm pretty sure I hate Lauren. Except when we're in the shower together. Then things are … complicated.

It's not like I can help it. I'm standing there on this narrow piece of plastic with no where else to look, getting splashed like a mouse who got too close to Jennifer Beals in Flashdance. And she's a giant. Of course I'm going to look. I start each shower telling myself that I'm going to be faithful to Tina, that I'm not going to even look at Lauren. I'm going to be a good girlfriend/pet.

Then Lauren puts her leg up on the side of the tub and rubs

shaving gel up and down her five story gams and I can see everything. Once you see something that magnificent and that intimate you can not take your eyes away.

I told you about how majestic Lauren looked just walking across the room. Take off the clothes and add water and you have a recipe for some very very impure thoughts. The kind of thoughts you enjoy while you're having them, but feel real shitty about when you think about the woman you love who isn't in them.

I have to admit there were a few times when Lauren caught me with my hands in the cookie jar if you catch my euphemism. At least here she could only douse me with shower water and not that damn spray bottle.

But back to me waking up early

I had no idea what time it was other than early. It might have been five minutes early or two hours. I had no way of knowing until the alarm went off and Lauren either got up or hit the snooze alarm. I couldn't see the clock from where I was. I wasn't strong enough to get out of the pet pocket on Lauren's bra.

Speaking of having sexual thoughts about Lauren, try camping out in Mammary Valley and not getting a case of lady wood. Before I got shrunk down I used to think that an A cup, like Lauren's, wasn't that impressive. I'd had a couple girlfriends that size who'd shown me how sensitive their little ladies could be, but the women who got my attention on the street tended to be a bit bustier.

At my new size I couldn't even fill one of Lauren's cups. Being strapped down like that meant that Lauren's little ladies towered over me in their white cotton containment. At least they were covered up.

I couldn't wait until Lauren and I were together and I could think all the sexy thoughts I wanted to about the woman I was sleeping with and showering with instead of feeling like I was cheating on her by wanting to rub one out to stupid sexy Lauren.

I lay back and forced myself to be patient. I really wasn't, patient that is, but there was nothing else I could do so I might as well pretend.

The steady rise and fall of Lauren's chest was soothing if I didn't think about it too much. I could almost fall back asleep, but Lauren said that today was going to be something special. Something about leaving the training area for the first time since I woke up in my bra. After so much time locked up with Lauren I was about as hyper as a three year old in a sugar factory. I wanted to know more about the trip, but Lauren misered the details like Scrooge rationed coal.

After two weeks cooped up with Attack of the Fifty Foot Dick, I was psyched.

The alarm finally went off and Lauren began her usual slow wake up.

"Good morning, Mistress Lauren. I hope you slept well last night." Lauren made me say that. She says it's important for me to remind her or Tina that I'm there, but I think Lauren just loves the smell of brown nosing in the morning.

"gwaddya rum." Lauren mumbled as she got out of bed and headed to the bathroom.

We went through the same morning routine we had for the past few weeks. Lauren snipped me out of my diapers, I did my business in the thimble toilet, we showered together (I tried to close my eyes, honest,) then I wrapped myself in a ginormous hand towel while Lauren dried and got dressed.

Being shrunk this small sucks. If I hadn't seen Tina that first day I'd just be stumbling around muttering that I should have listened to Carly. Knowing that I have Tina to look forward to makes up for life under the Lauren regime. But there is one thing that I truly love about being this small.

That hand towel.

No, I'm not shitting you. This thing is the most amazingly soft towel that I have ever had the pleasure of drying myself off on. And it's bigger than most bedspread. Some mornings I'd just cocoon myself dry rolling myself up in it and pretending I was Cleopatra getting delivered to Marc Anthony. Only a girl Marc Anthony. Marcia Antonia?

Everything was normal. My new normal anyway. I was snuggling up in my ginormous towel feeling like the Queen of Denial when Lauren dropped a teeny tiny stack of clothes just a couple feet from where I was. Me sized clothes. I pulled myself out of the towel and crawled on all fours to inspect my unexpected present.

"For me?" I looked up at Lauren giving her my most adorable puppy dog eyes.

"Don't thank me, it was Tina's orders. She doesn't want you strutting around naked when she takes you out. So I have to make sure you get dressed before I take you anywhere. Even around the compound. I've got a lot of things to go over with you before we leave. You have five minutes to pull up your big girl panties or we're not going."

"Yes, Mistress Lauren."

After weeks of enforced day time nudity I was fucking giddy at the chance to put on some real clothes for a change. And these were real clothes, not Barbie's hand-me-downs.

I put on the bra first. I'd spent way too much time flopping around like I was in a National Geographic documentary and my girls were aching for some support. By tonight I'd be ready to throw it across the room, but for right now it was damn welcome.

The bra and the underwear were a matched set in white cotton. They did their job, but they weren't as sexy as I normally would have gone for. Good quality, but a bit plain. But I wasn't going to complain about it. It wasn't like I was wearing it for anyone else. As long as it covered my butt I was happy as a clam.

The dress was super cute. Also a tad conservative, but there was something about the style that just worked for me in a way the undies hadn't. It was powder blue, buttoned up the front, and came down to my knees. It fit like dream.

"I feel like I walked off the set of Mad Men." I said as I twirled around. My skirt flew higher and higher.

"Get your shoes on, Betty Draper. I don't have all day."

I fell straight back onto my giant towel then gathered up the cute ankle socks and low heeled pumps that completed my ensemble.

"Do I look as cute and dainty as I feel?" I climbed up Lauren's toothbrush holder to check myself out in the mirror. "Why yes, I believe I do."

"That's great, but stop doing that and pay attention. I need to show you how this works."

Lauren placed a purse on the sink not too far from where I was. I must have been getting used to being so small because when I saw it my first thought was "purse" and not "tent like leather house."

"I know how a purse works, Lauren."

"What happens if you need to go to the bathroom while you're out and about in one of these?"

"I ... hold it?"

"How many hours can you do that?"

"Not many." I admitted.

"Then I need to show you how to use this or you're going to be peeing all over Tina's lip gloss."

"There's a toilet in there?"

"Sort of."

"Do all purses have toilets in them or is this a special thing? If my lipstick could pee would it have had a place to do it? Enquiring minds want to know, Lauren."

"Stop being weird and listen. If you don't learn I'll just put you in a pair of dolly diapers and forget about it. Do you want me to put you in dolly diapers? Do you want that?"

"I'll listen. Just stop saying 'dolly diapers. OK.'"

Twenty minutes later we were on our way.

Lauren looked a little weird walking around carrying a nice Italian leather handbag dressed in her jeans and a Dokken t-shirt, but I was more focused on seeing the world outside the training area from my perch in said stylish leather handbag.

I'm not exactly a font of wisdom. I'm pretty sure that there are some people who might even question my sanity after all the things I gave up and what I had done to myself to be with a woman I'd never even technically said "hello" to. But they never heard of love.

There is one thing that I can say with all certainty, being carried in a purse is light years better than being carried around in some giant's sweaty fist. Maybe there's a little more jostling, but you can close your eyes and pretend that you're riding on one of those cable gondolas up the side of some Swiss mountain.

The trip outside the training area seemed surreal. Lauren casually walked down the hallways exposing me to more and more people. Most ignored me, but some gave me a look or a condescending smile as they walked by. None of them interacted with me. The more people I saw the less I thought of myself as normal. When it was just Lauren and me I could fool myself into thinking that she was the freak. Explaining away the giant Lincoln logs took a bit more mental gymnastics, but it was still pretty easy to think that I'd been captured by some experiment who had escaped her mad scientist.

Seeing a dozen giants towering over my little head shattered that sad illusion pretty quick.

The halls themselves were pretty dull. At my size they were vast caverns going on forever, but that awe faded away pretty quick. Lauren paused by a window while she waited for an elevator and I got my first look at the outside.

Between the window and the distance the outside world looked normal to me. Like I could hop out of the purse, walk outside, and be my old size again walking underneath the trees reaching up to grab twigs off the lowest branches.

Then a leaf as big as I was blew against the glass right in front of me. The wind held it there long enough to destroy that illusion too. I was small and weak and if I went outside I'd probably get carried away by a chipmunk. Like any other nut.

We went up to the third floor. The number didn't mean anything to me, it was just the button Lauren pressed once the elevator doors were closed.

"What's on the third floor?" I asked after we started moving.

"The pet shop."

"Puppies or kitties? Don't tell me it's fish. I always feel so sad for them, trapped their in their little glass worlds."

"None of the above." Lauren said. "These are the resizeds who didn't get bought."

"Cause they changed their minds?"

"Or their supposed to be owners didn't want them after they shrank. Yeah."

"Why the field trip?"

"New management directives. We're supposed to show ready to graduate resizeds how bad things can be for those who just say 'no.'"

"I'm not saying no. That's just silly. I'd never do that to Tina. Or me."

"Whatever. Just look at the freaks, act all forlorn, and I'll get you back home before too long."

"Yes, Mistress Lauren." I replied. "Did you say I was close to graduating?"

"Closer than not."

"A couple days closer or a couple weeks closer?"

"That would be telling."

The elevator dinged before I could beat any more information out of Lauren.

The littlest people pet shop smelled like a vet's office. That same stuff they put in the air to keep the animals calm. Or something.

Lauren was greeted at the door by some guy in a goatee who was even taller than she was and wore a white lab coat over his Nirvana t-shirt. They kissed their hellos. It was a lengthy greeting. I suppose if I were dating Lauren I'd want to keep her mouth too busy to talk also.

"Why don't you drop her off in the play area and I can show you around out back." Goatee boy said. "Muriel can watch over her."

"Sounds perfect." Lauren said. "Did you bring the ..."

"Of course."

I'm not sure what was going on between them, but I quickly found myself dropped off in the middle of a small city. A city not so much on a hill as one of those small plastic play tables that are all the rage in the toddler set. And not so much made out of concrete and steel as legos and kids' letter blocks.

And I was not alone.

"You two have fun." I called out to their retreating backs. They weren't paying me any attention. "I'll just hang out here until you're done. And I can go back to that great great training."

Physically I was waving them off, but what I was really doing was delaying the inevitable. I really didn't want to meet any more tiny people. Especially not tiny people who didn't have a Tina to take them home. I felt bad enough for me, I didn't need to have a whole new bunch of people to care about.

I was just turning around to face my shrunken peers when I caught a glimpse of something huge barreling towards me. Before I could say WTF I was picked up off the ground and pressed hard into a giant Q letter block. I'd been picked up and manhandled a lot lately, but there was something different about this time. I looked up to the sky to see what giant had done this to me only there wasn't anyone standing there. Which made no kind of sense. My feet were way off the ground and I could feel myself being held by the neck by a pair of giant fingers.

I lowered my gaze until I saw who really was holding me up. It was another shrunken woman. Only she wasn't as shrunk as I was.

She was a blond haired blue eyed glamazon who must have been four times as tall as me. About the size of a Barbie doll; and it looked like she raided Barb's wardrobe. And she looked pissed.

"That's a mighty nice dress you're wearing, meat." Bizarro Barbie hissed in my face. "I bet you think you're better than me cause you got real clothes. I bet you think it'll help you get adopted before me."

I started to say something, but she put her left hand right over my throat and used her other to reach under my dress. With all my weight being supported on my throat I wasn't able to breathe let alone talk. If I weighed what I normally weighed she probably would have crushed my wind pipe.

I heard sounds of other people calling out to this mini-giant, but I couldn't make out what they were saying. I felt her reach up and start to yank off my underwear. I tried to kick her, but it was like kicking a meat statue. She pulled my underwear off, tossed them to the ground, and proceeded to shuck my shoes and socks off.

Then she let go.

I fell only a few inches, but as far as I was concerned it was closer to a two story drop. I landed in a heap at her feet. I felt her huge hands reach down and take mine. At first I thought she was trying to help me to my feet, but she was just getting my arms into position to pull my dress up over my head. But the dress didn't come off like that so it winded up getting stuck around my neck. I thought that huge bitch was going to rip my head off trying to get my dress over my noggin, but she left it covering my face and turned her attention to ripping off my bra.

Naked from the neck down and blinded by my own dress I stumbled backwards. The blonde bitch let my dress fall down far enough for her to rip the buttons enough to get it all the way off. She grabbed the rest of my discarded clothing and stuffed everything under her arm.

"You are not getting adopted before me, meat."

The blonde placed her fist right up to my face. The fist was bigger. She pulled it back and brought it down hard on my chest. The next thing I knew I was looking up from the ground. She was walking away.

"She punched me in the boob." I said. "She stole my clothes and punched me in the boob."

"I'm sorry you had to go through that." A woman about my size said. "Let me help you up then we'll see about getting you a tissue."

"That's ok, I don't feel like crying." I said, taking her hand and getting unsteadily to my feet.

"Not for crying, to wear. Like a toga." The woman explained. "Unless you'd rather spend the rest of the day naked."

"Don't feel you have to get dressed on our account. We're real laid back here." I had to look down to see the dude who said that. He was about half my size.

"Hush, Walter. She's already freaking out enough without you having to scare her too." The woman let go of me once I was fully on my feet. "I'm Paige. The little perv is Walter. Welcome to the pet shop."

"I'm Becky. Nice to meet you, Paige. Toulouse Lauperv." I nodded down at Walter. "That tissue sounds great."

I did my best to cover myself. Paige gave Walter a gentle slap on the back of the head to keep his eyes from perving out and he ratcheted down the sleeze.

Paige led us to one of the Lego buildings. We passed about a dozen other shrunken people on the way there. Mostly men, but a few women sprinkled in here and there. I must have been a popular size;

most everyone looked about normal to me. Walter and the blonde bitch were the only outliers I could see.

None of the other shrunken people said or did anything to me.

We got inside and sat me down on a makeshift chair that used to be a yogurt container while Paige searched for something for me to cover up with. The container was cold on my bare butt, but it did keep Walter from staring at it.

"My eyes are up here." I told him."

"I'll have to take your word for it; I can't see that far up."

"Shut up, Walter or I'll kick you out."

"It feels good talking to someone my size again." I said, to Paige. "I thought all my conversations were going to end with a stiff neck from looking up so long."

"Are you coming here to be adopted or are they trying to scare you into saying yes?" Paige asked, handing me my tissue toga.

"Scared straight. That's me. Not that they need to, I'm definitely saying yes. I love Tina and there's nothing that they can do to stop us from being together." I wrapped the tissue around my body like a towel.

"Why do all the hot ones have to be gay." Walter grumbled at my knee. "Or psychotic."

"I hope everything goes smoothly on Tina's end." Paige said.

"Speaking of psychotic, what's the deal with the blonde bus that attacked me?"

"That's Lisa." Walter said. "She's a return."

"They have a return policy? On people?"

"Mostly, no." Paige said. "They made an exception for Lisa."

"Besides, Lisa's not people." Walter said.

"None of us are anymore."

"So how'd you two end up here?" I needed to change the subject.

"I met this amazing woman and made the mistake of telling her my deepest fantasy." Walter said. "She got my money and decided she'd rather spend it on a yacht than buying me. I here she even tried to get a refund on the shrinking."

"I'm sorry."

"Right now I'm just hoping that whoever does buy me isn't too weird. You should see some of the nut jobs that pass as customers here.

"It gets weirder than this?" I looked around at the … everything about this place.

"For a whole lot of people, getting shrunk is just step one." Paige said. "Shrinking, or having someone who is shrunk, is a gateway to a whole new realm of …"

"Weirdos."

"Lucky I have Tina."

"I said the same thing about, Samantha." Walter said.

"What about you, Paige. Did some guy … or gal do you wrong too?"

"Nothing like that. In fact I'm not even a macrophile."

"That makes two of us. What are you, then?"

"An ethnologist."

"One. I thought you were going to say something way different than that. Two. What's an ethnologist doing in Candyland?"

"I study cultures. Mostly through the lens of history, but not always. We have an emerging culture right here and I wanted to be the first to study it up close."

"So you got yourself shrunk and volunteered to be kenneled by the Inhumane Society?"

"The plan was for me to be resized and then purchased through a grant I'd obtained. A colleague of mine was going to be my official 'owner.' I would then travel the country, eventually the world, getting case histories of other resized individuals."

"I'm betting there's an 'only something went wrong' in there."

"There was just one thing that I had overlooked."

"When she stopped being a person she lost her grant money." Walter finished. He'd obviously heard the story before.

"With no grant money Thomas wasn't able to buy me. With my potential buyer out of the picture I ended up here."

"I am so sorry."

"It could be worse. So far the really extreme customers haven't shown any interest in me and I'm able to interact with other resizeds on a level I never imagined I'd find myself at."

"Fellow slave?"

Paige shrugged her shoulders.

"So tell me about these weirdo buyers. What are they like? Do they …"

A thunder clap interrupted what I was about to say.

"WTF?"

"That's Muriel. She always does that to get our attention when customers are in the pet shop. You want to find out about the weirdos, lady. You're about to see 'em."

"I'm sorry, Becky, we're not allowed to stay out of sight when we have that sort of company. You're not for sale so you can stay here if you'd like, but Walter and I don't have a choice. We can talk later, assuming no one buys me."

"That is the saddest thing I've heard since I got here. I'll come with. Maybe I'll be your good luck charm and you won't get bought."

The sky was full of giants when we walked outside. The toy city we were stranded in blocked most of the horizon, but we could see there were at least half a dozen people looking down at us or passing in and out of our limited view.

We hadn't gotten too far when I spied something on the other side of the square that pissed me right the fuck off.

"That bitch is wearing my dress. The pretty one I was traumatically ripped out of. Why is she wearing my dress?"

"That's Lola." Walter said, as if that explained everything.

"Lola's one of Lisa's lackeys. Lisa probably gave her your dress as a present."

"Well I want it back."

I started to cross the square, but Paige put her hand on my shoulder.

"Not now." She said. "If you cause a commotion while buyers are here then everyone gets punished. Just wait until this is over and I'll see if I can convince Lola to give you the dress back."

"OK." I was still pissed, but didn't want to get the class in trouble. "So how does this work?"

"It's a fish tank, Becky and we're the guppies." Walter said. "We just swim around here where the people can see us. If they like what they see they scoop us up and take a closer look."

"Only they don't throw us back if we're too small." Paige added.

"That's horrible."

"That's life. Our lives. I just wonder what will happen when Stovent decides to start breeding us."

"What?!"

"Resizeds are a slave race. It's the next logical step."

"The shrunken people signed away their rights. Their baby can't." I said.

"Neither parent is human; how can the offspring expect human rights?"

"That's evil."

"That's life."

"Her, the one with the big tits in the toga. I want to see her." A giant man towering above us pointed straight at me.

"Me?"

I pointed at my chest, but he wasn't paying me any attention. He was speaking to a woman in a suit who I assumed was Muriel.

"He doesn't mean me." I said to Paige. "She knows I'm not for sale."

Paige was about to tell me something when a giant hand reached out of the sky and plucked me out of the toy city. When I finally stopped moving I found myself standing on a wooden table with a giant blonde man staring down at me. He was seated. Standing behind him was Muriel.

"Do you know who I am?" I called up to Muriel.

"I know precisely what you are, little girl. Now be polite to Mr. Saunders."

"Ohhh. I get it. This is part of the tour. I get to talk to the pets and find out how bad they have it, then I come up here and get drooled over by some Dennis Hopper wannabe. I get it. You're not even a real buyer are you?"

"Clearly there is a reason why this one is here." Saunders said.

"Some of the resizeds have their rough edges." Muriel said. "This one more than most. Some men enjoy that kind of challenge."

"Take off your toga." The giant dick ordered, bending in closer. His breath smelled disgusting.

"No!"

"What do you mean 'no?'"

Something in me snapped. After weeks of being polite to a sadist who had the hotline to my one true love. After being physically beaten and stripped less than a minute after being brought here. After seeing the only day clothes I'd been allowed in weeks on some skank who kissed the ass of the woman who beat me. I was not about to take any shit from some actor who was paid to make me make the choice I was going to make anyway.

"I mean you are not seeing my goodies, Mr. Pickle Breath. And if you reach over here and try to take this toga off my stunning body I will climb up your arm, down your pants, and I will beat your balls with my mighty little fists. If you think for one second that just cause you're bigger than me you get to assault me whenever and however you like than you are even dumber than you look."

"I've seen enough." Pickle Breath left in a huff, Muriel in hot pursuit.

"So have I."

I turned my head and saw another giant. She was resting her chin on the table and staring right at me. She wore her hair in bangs and had these intense eyes. I'd have called her cute if I wasn't so god damned pissed off.

"Lady, the same thing I said to him goes double for you. Only instead of your balls I will crawl up inside you and use your ovaries as punching bags."

Muriel came back. She was almost as pissed as I was.

"She's perfect." The giant with the bangs said. "I'll take her."

"How much are you offering?" Muriel's anger was ramping down at the prospect of a commission. Only there shouldn't be a commission cause these were just actors. Right?

I almost peed my toga when mystery woman said how much.

"But I'm not for sale." I said. "I belong to Tina. OK, I will belong to Tina. I'm only visiting on the scared straight program. Just ask goatee boy. Or Lauren."

"Is that true?" Bang woman almost looked like she was about to cry.

"Little Lola here is lying. She must have heard about the visitor we had today."

"LOLA? Are you blind, bitch?"

"Our visitor is wearing a powder blue dress. You are not, Lola."

"Jesus H. Christ! Do we all look the fucking same to you?"

"There will be no trouble buying Lola today, Ms. Brewster."

"LISTEN TO ME YOU FUCKING C …"

I think she shoved a cotton ball in my face. All I know is I was cut off mid-tirade by a face full of soft and white. I smelled something sweet and the white turned to black and nothing else mattered.

Six: Whatever Lola Wants

I woke up fast to a slow room.

I don't know what they used on me, but it didn't leave a headache. If you're gonna get drugged by enormously powerful giants I suppose that's the way to go. Hallucinations did seem to be on the list of side effects though. But that was alright.

I was in a huge bed. And by huge I mean scaled for me king-sized, not a twin bed that looked like a football field. The sheets were silk and the pillows were the stuff that dreams were made of. The room around me was my sized and had a desk, and dressers, and a door, and none of it looked like doll furniture. And I hand't been sleeping in a dolly diaper.

I liked this hallucination.

The nightgown was so silky I didn't even know I was wearing it until I pulled myself out of the sheets. It looked like something Ginger Rogers would have worn to bed after nightclubbing with Fred. On the one hand I should have felt super creeped out that they had dressed me while I was drugged off my ass. On the other hand I had been wearing the most disposable clothing possible. Maybe they sneezed. I called it a wash and got out of bed.

"Hello." I called out to the room. "In case anyone's monitoring me, I'm alive and hallucinating. Or you're effing with my head again. Either way just thought you should know."

If anyone was listening to me they didn't say.

"Okay then. I'll just look around the room until you decide to show yourselves. And I'm assuming that the whole mix up between me and Lola got sorted out. Cause only Tina gets to buy me."

Still nothing. So I checked the room.

It was perfect. So perfect that I was pretty sure my weeks under Lauren's regime had been a hugely bad dream. Like someone had slipped crack into my coffee. There was good stationery in the desk. And an inkwell. And the kind of pen that used an inkwell. There was a vanity with high end cosmetics. A closet full of amazing clothes. An en-suite bathroom.

I almost cried when saw a toilet I could use.

"Am I dead?" I asked out loud again. "And is this going to go all Twilight Zone and it turns out I think I'm in Heaven, but I'm really in

Hell? Cause those episodes suck."

Still no answer.

I opened the last door and found a hallway.

"I am totally going to see where this leads, but not in my nighty. And not without washing the stank off first. Unless this really is Hell and the plumbing doesn't work."

But everything worked. I had plenty of hot water for my bath. And the shower I took to wash off all the bath gels and wash my hair.

I combed my hair and did my makeup for the first time in forever. The clothes were … wow. I could have spent all day going through the wardrobe, but I was starting to feel hungry and the room hadn't come with a mini-fridge. I settled for a pair of black slacks, a blue button down blouse, and a pair of matching flats to do my exploring in.

Then I noticed the phone. An old elegant landline that looked like something Rita Hayworth used for phone sex back in the day. I'd seen it before when I was looking around the room, but my brain didn't make the connection. A phone like that had to be for show; more people used carrier pigeons than landlines.

I picked it up and put the receiver to my ear.

There was a dial tone!

All I had to do was remember Carly's phone number and I could … OK a specific plan wasn't coming, but it would at least be good to talk to her again.

Of course, I couldn't remember her number. Or any of my old co-workers. Or my ex-girlfriend. And I never even had Tina's number. All of those (except for Tina's) were on my smart phone. I just hit an icon and they were talking to me. I never needed to manually input the number again. I wasn't a savage for god's sake.

I ended up dialing O. Lucky for me I'd watched enough olde time movies to know how to work a rotary dial phone. The phone rang three times before I heard someone pick up.

"Hello. This is Rebecca Hogarth. I need the telephone number of Carly Vint …"

"Good, you'e awake." A woman's voice interrupted me.

"Yeesss. You're not the operator are you?"

"No."

"You know what's going on?"

"More than you do. And I thought your name was Lola."

Fuck! She thought I was that skank. That was a really really bad sign.

"Just tell me you're not the devil."

"You must be getting hungry." She laughed when she spoke.

"You didn't answer my question, but yeah, I am feeling a bit peckish."

"My name's Maria, not Lucifer. If you want to eat you'll have to come up here."

"Where's 'here?'"

"When you leave your room take a left. That'll lead you to an elevator. It only goes between your floor and here."

"Alright."

"But before you come up you should do some exploring. There's something down there that we need to talk about and it'll be easier if you've seen it first."

"Can you vague that up for me some more?"

She hung up.

"This is how bad horror movies get started." I said out loud. I'm not sure why. "Maybe I'm just freaking out."

I headed out the door and hung a left. There was an elevator. There was also a whole lot more corridor going off around the corner. I wished I had a weapon. Or could MacGyver a flame thrower out of hair spray and a match. Or that I had a match.

I passed the elevator and kept on going down the hallway and around the corner. That's when I came to the stair well. I wasn't sure if I was supposed to go up, down, or stay on this level so I just kept walking forward and hoped that I'd find whatever it was Maria wanted me to find and that it wouldn't eat me.

At least I saw plenty of signs pointing me back to the elevator; I didn't have any breadcrumbs to drop.

The weird thing (aside from everything) was the fact that there were no other doors. Just the one to my room, the elevator, and the one for the stairwell. There wasn't even a janitor's closet.

"Just walking around, hoping not to get killed. That's why I hated D&D. And the Dungeon Master who kept trying to look down my shirt. But mostly the lethal walking."

I kept walking. Then I did some more walking. After I walked some more I turned a corner and the wall on my right was replaced with a floor to ceiling window.

I was looking into some sort of hangar. It was brightly lit. I could see some sort of dirty tarp covering something huge, but I couldn't make out what it was. This had to be what Maria was talking about. I needed to figure out what was in there then I could go upstairs for breakfast and explanations.

I kept on walking, trying to get a better angle on whatever it was, but all I saw was the same crappy tarp. I made it halfway across the hangar before I saw its face.

Her face.

The woman with the bangs who tried to buy me.

Staring right at me with those gorgeous sad eyes.

shitfuckshit

She did buy me. That idiot Muriel couldn't tell me from Lola and Lauren was too busy bonking her boyfriend in the supply closet to say anything so I got sold to bang lady and now I was never going to be with Tina ever again.

I backed myself against the wall and went full fetal position. Any second now that window was going to swing open and a giant hand was going to pull me inside and some weirdo would do unspeakable things to me and there was nothing I could do to stop it.

But nothing happened.

I looked up to see bang woman staring forward, but not right at me.

"Can you see me?" I asked, uncoiling my arms and waving my hands in the air.

She didn't even blink.

"I've got a bad feeling about this."

I walked up to the glass. Her eyes didn't track my movement. I took a good long look. Now that I knew I was looking at a person it made some things easier to identify. I could see that she was kneeling on her hands and feet. What I thought was a tarp turned out to be a raggy dress. There wasn't much of it, but what there was looked itchy and filthy. It didn't look like she had room to stand or even move around that much. I didn't see anything for her to entertain herself with. Books, phone, TV. She was just kneeling there in next to nothing. And that next to nothing looked like something two dogs fought over.

"What the fuck."

My head was too full of questions for my body to stand still so I paced all the elevator ride up to Maria.

The door dinged open and I strode out onto a giant table in the middle of a giant kitchen. All of a sudden I was no longer normal. Like the elevator ride had shrunk me. Sure, I'd seen a giant woman kneeling five minutes ago, but she was in an airplane hangar. Or something that looked like one. And I was in a nice normal hallway. In the world on the other side of this elevator she was the aberration. Up here I was the freak.

"I set up a table for you on the other side of the sugar bowl. Take a seat and I'll get your plate ready. I've got coffee brewed, but I can make tea if you'd prefer."

The voice was attached to a giant woman. Maybe 30. Wearing jeans and a nice blouse.

"Maria?"

"I sure ain't the devil."

"Breakfast sounds great, but there's been a huge mixup. Muriel's either blind or she's some kind of size racist. … Sizeist? … Anyway, I'm not Lola. I have someone who wants to buy me and I really really want to belong to them and we can't be together if I'm here. And the woman who brought me here is downstairs looking like the Goodyear blimp version of those Gor novels my ex-girlfriend Jillian was super into. And this couldn't feel more like Silence of the Lambs if you lowered a bucket of lotion down the elevator shaft."

"Sit down and eat; I'm going to need my coffee for this."

"But …"

Maria walked out of view before I could talk sense into her.

I found the table Maria had told me about. High quality. Like the furnishings in my room. Definitely not doll furniture. It even had me-sized silverware and a cloth napkin. I took a seat and waited for food and answers.

"It's not practical to shrink your food so I made you a plate from mine. I hope you don't mind. And you seem a bit wired already so I went with OJ instead of caffeine. If you talk any faster I'm not going to be able to hear you."

"Thank you."

The situation was shitty, but at least Maria was being nice to me. And the food smelled amazing. She waited for me to dig in before pouring herself a cup of coffee and taking a seat facing me. Her coffee cup was bigger than me.

"I'm not sure how this is going to come out. There's a lot to unpack and this is almost as weird for me as it is for you. So please be patient."

"Okay." I said between bites of bacon.

"You really are Rebecca and not Lola?"

"Cross my heart." And I did.

"That makes this complicated."

"If you're looking for a place to start, how about the woman downstairs?"

"That's Jordan Brewster. She used to be one of the 30 richest people in the country."

"And now she's kneeling in a box. What's up with that? Enquiring minds want to know."

"Jordan is submissive. Sexually. She brought you here to be her domme." Maria took a sip of coffee to wash down that bombshell.

"… but how … why? She owns me. Doesn't she?"

"Part of Jordan's fantasy is to get shoved down the social ladder. Being controlled by someone from a lower rung gets her going. I used to be her housemaid until she sold herself to me."

"She's your slave?"

"We signed a contract. It's not legal. Not like the way I own you."

"Jordan bought me, but you own me?"

"Ah ha." Another sip of coffee. "The slave contract may have been pretend, but the papers transferring all her money and holdings over to me were real enough. She can't touch a dime unless I open the purse strings."

"So lets see if I get this straight. She wants me to be the littlest dominatrix cause she thinks she's going to get off being ordered around by Tom Thumb's little sister?"

"You are easily the least powerful human being in history. And her former maid owns you. Making her the slave of a pet of someone who used to fetch her dry cleaning."

"I have to say I find that a little insulting, but I'm going to move on and ask you why you let her buy me? If you control the cash why spend that much money on me. I heard what you paid. I'm not worth it."

"She wasn't getting what she needed from me. When she found out about Stovent she considered getting resized. Then she got it in her head that being topped by a tiny was just what she was looking for. Convinced me to build her voyeur dungeon and your apartment. But she never found anyone who she thought could dominate her. Real dommes didn't want to be shrunk and bought. And the abandoned tinies in the pet shop were all too submissive to do what she wanted. She'd visited the pet shop half a dozen times over the last year. When she saw you in action she begged me to release the funds to buy you. And I did."

"Are you in love with her?"

"I love her, but I'm not in love with her. I'm not gay. Neither is she, supposedly."

"But it sounds like you two …" I let the innuendo fade to grey.

"Yeah, but my heart wasn't in it. I only did it to please her and she could tell. It's part of why she picked you."

"She does know that I'm a woman, right? Cause if she doesn't and she's not gay that sounds like a great excuse to bring me back."

"Jordan comes from a pretty conservative background. I think she's in denial about a lot of things. Being 'made' to be with a woman plays into her fantasies while giving her a safe way to explore her sexuality."

"Well I am a gay woman and I'm in love with another lesbian. There's been a huge mistake. Just bring me back and we can find another tiny lady to boss Jordan around. I know this stone cold bitch named Lisa who'd be perfect for the job."

"Jordan has her heart set on you."

"And I had my heart set on a puppy, but Santa shit the bed."

"But the puppy's here. And she's already seen it. It would be cruel to not let her play with it."

"She gets off on cruel. This is being cruel to me and I don't enjoy it."

"That's why it's complicated."

"It's not. Just look into your heart and do the right thing. You seem like a nice lady, Maria. Please, don't turn out to be an asshole."

Jordan took a long swig of her coffee as she looked down at my pleading face.

"I tell you what. You give Jordan what she wants and I'll think about getting you to your girlfriend. Deal?"

"I don't have a choice, do I?"

"No."

"Alright." I took a deep breath. "Tell me Jordan's fantasies. Every detail you can think of. If I'm gonna do this I need to do it right.

I let the click clack click of my stiletto heels announce my presence as I wordlessly strode into Jordan's hangar/kennel. Her eyes are on me from the second the door flips open and don't leave me as I cross over to her. It's a little walk for me, but there is barely any room for the giant slave to move around in.

Maria tried to convince me to come in here in full dominatrix drag, but that wasn't going to happen. There wasn't enough talcum powder in the world to get me into some of the outfits Jordan expected her dolly domme to wear. I agreed to the heels cause they were amazing and went with a simple black one piece swimsuit that showed enough flesh to be interesting. Not that Jordan could see it under the Jedi cloak I was wearing. Jordan couldn't even see my face with the hood up.

I clicked over to the wall opposite Jordan. I could feel the weight of her stare as I inspected the rack of bondage equipment laid out for my use. Some was normal sized, others were miniaturized versions of the real thing. Jordan sure did give me options.

"Do you know who I am?" I asked. I was still facing the whips and chains, but I pulled the hood of my cloak down.

"You are Mistress Lola." I could hear the submissive need in her voice.

I pulled the largest me-sized bullwhip from the rack. It was officially showtime.

CRACK!

"Wrong!"

I wasn't facing her, but I could feel Jordan stiffen at the crack of my voice and whip. If I didn't have her complete attention before, I had it now.

"I had a very interesting conversation with Maria." I turned to face her the whip still in my tiny hands. "She can't be bothered with you anymore. She's got your money. Your cars. This house. She's taken you for every thing that you owned or ever will own and put you in a kennel like the bitch you are."

Jordan was kneeling on all fours with her head level with her butt. Her lower legs were flat against the cold tile floor and her thighs shot up to her hips in a straight line. She couldn't have been com-fortable in that position, but it was the most comfortable she could be.

I walked towards her still carrying the whip. Her eyes followed me until I walked under her head and out of sight. I wasn't entirely surrounded by Jordan's body, but it sure did feel like I had walked into a cave of her. Her forearms rose like pillars behind me. I could see her chest heave with each breath far above my head.

"Maria has a new pet now. Me. And she loves me more than she ever loved you. You know what she did to show me how much she loves me? Do you? She told me that I could have anything I wanted. Anything within her power. And you know what I chose?

"You."

I strolled to the other side of the Jordan cave and ran the whip along her thighs.

"I'm three inches tall in my stocking feet. Hummingbirds outweigh me. I'm not even a person anymore. I'm just a talking pet that can walk on her hind legs. But none of that matters because you belong to me. Now lose the dress; I want to inspect my property.

There wasn't much to the dress, but there wasn't much to the room either. Jordan struggled to pull the dress off without crushing me under her. I watched as first one then two giant breasts were pulled out of the filthy ratty excuse for a dress. Then the dress was pulled down her back and was pushed down her legs past her feet. I doubted she could put it back on now, but mostly I wasn't thinking about that. I was looking at labia the size of a door glistening in the indirect light.

"Nice stalactites." I said, turning my attention away from her arousal to the giant breasts that hung over my head. Her nipples looked almost painfully erect. I had no doubt that Jordan was living her fantasy.

"Now back to your mistake about my name and title. My name is not Lola, it's Rebecca. And the term 'Mistress' has become too gender fucked to describe anyone as fabulous as me. You can call me Goddess Rebecca or you can just call me Goddess. Do you understand?"

"Yes, Goddess Rebecca."

"Such a good girl. Such a smart girl. And what are you called?"

"Jordan, Goddess Rebecca."

CRACK!

The bullwhip snaked upwards to its full length and hit the bullseye of her dangling left nipple. Her entire body jerked in reaction to the sudden unexpected sting. Her arm jerked and I thought she was going to shield her tender boobs with it, but that was just reflex action. Her masochistic force of will kept her arm down and her naked flesh vulnerable.

She held her position. And moaned.

"Let's see if you can learn." I said. "What are you called?"

"Whatever you want to call me, my Goddess."

"Absolutely right." I could already see a small welt forming on her whipped nipple. "Since you like 'Lola' so much why don't we call you that. Can you say your new name slave?"

" … lola …"

CRACK!

The whip kissed her other nipple.

"Say it like you mean it or the next one lands on your clit."

"My name is Lola. Goddess Rebecca gave me that name. It is beautiful and I love it and I love my Goddess and I pray that I will be her property forever and ever."

"Promises. Promises."

I spent the next few minutes just walking around under the newly christened Lola. She still couldn't see me, but she could hear the click clack of my heels as I walked a circuit around her and feel the gentle teasing of my hands and whip as I touched the parts of her I could reach. Her breathing grew deeper pushing her breasts closer and closer to me. Her nipples looked like they were trying to stab me.

"Are you enjoying this, Lola? Being on display for your new pint sized owner?"

" … yes …"

"What about the whipping. Did you enjoy that?" I ran the edge of the whip along the underside of her wrist.

" … yes …" Her giant body shivered at my touch.

"Is Lola my little pain slut?"

"Lola is Goddess Rebecca's pain slut."

"You used to be someone, Lola. You used to be the one in charge giving orders and spending money from that huge bank account of yours. Now you're kneeling in a kennel in the very lowest part of the house you used to own. The woman who used to wash your floors now sleeps in your bed while you drink out of a dog bowl. The woman who used to serve your breakfast in bed is now spending your money. Correction. Her money. You don't own anything anymore do you?"

" … no …"

"Not even your dress. Why don't you tell me where that came from."

"Bertie. The gardner. He found two dogs fighting over a rag. Maria let me use it as a dress." I couldn't see her face, but I could hear the blush in her voice.

"I'm a god damned purse pet and I live better than you. I'm not even a human being and I have more freedom than you. I am nothing, but I am better than you."

Her breathing was getting even heavier.

"Does that make my little Lola hot?"

"It makes me very hot, my Goddess."

"That's pathetic. You're pathetic."

I stopped by her right hand.

"You've been touching yourself, haven't you? Don't lie. I can smell it on your dirty paws."

"Yes, Goddess Rebecca."

"When you're down here in your kennel. Alone. Forgotten. Rubbing one out cause that's all you're good for. Do you think about little ol' me coming down here and cracking the whip?"

"Yes."

"Then today's Lola's lucky day."

I walked out from under her naked kneeling body. I left the whip under her; I'd be needing it later. Her eyes were laser focused on me as I walked over to the toy wall and made my next selection.

It didn't take long for me to find what I was looking for. To a normal woman the nipple clamps would have looked scary enough; at my size they were a couple bear traps held together by a long chain.

I let the cloak drop to the floor giving Lola a good look at my swimsuit clad body.

"Does Lola like what she sees?"

Lola could only nod.

"I like what I see too."

I tossed the clamps over my shoulder. I felt the cold metal bounce against my back as I wrapped a piece of the long chain around my wrist for support. I felt like I was a French Canadian trapper headed out to the Yukon as I walked back under Lola and into the flesh cave her crouching body had formed. I stopped at her right hand. The one she had used to jill off. I placed one than two clamps on top of it and slowly poured the chain down on top of it.

"I'm not strong enough to pull these open, but you're big and strong and have to do everything that I tell you to. Just a big dumb animal. Put them on, pet and make sure the chain is straight. I'm going to teach you your first trick."

No matter what she did Lola was unable to see her own breasts. The ceiling was too low for her to sit up straight and get a good view of her bodacious ta tas and she couldn't bend her neck enough to look straight down at her chest. To make things even more fun she had to balance her weight with her arms. She managed to keep herself steady with one while the other blindly grabbed a nipple and applied the clamp, but it was a real production. I heard her let out a sharp squeal when the metal teeth dug into her already abused nipple.

I found my arms protectively going up to my own boobs in sympathy for what she was going through. Lucky for me Lola couldn't see that; according to Maria my new pet needed a stone cold bitch to get off to. And if I was ever going to see Tina again I'd have to make Lola happy.

"The chains not straight. Take them off and try again." I was being a dick, but I was being a dick for love.

It took three more attempts and a lot of sexy moans from my slave before she got the clamps on exactly as I wanted them. I looked up at the two giant breasts staring down from me from the ceiling of her flesh. There were fresh red marks around the places where the clamps were … clamped. From her earlier failures. The long gold chain dangled between each breast. If I jumped I might just be able to reach it, but I didn't need to jump.

"Good girl. Now lower your boobs until I tell you to stop."

A pair of giant breasts slowly descended from the sky. Just like in my sexy Star Wars trash compactor fantasy. When the chain dangled down to my butt level I ordered her to stop. I got up on my tippy toes and slid my butt down onto the chain. The clamped nipples pulled at the weight and I heard a faint mew from Lola as I sat my tiny but full mass down on the chain. It may not have been much, but it was enough to make the part of the chain I was sitting on droop even further down. If I stretched I could just touch her breasts and I had a perfect view of her crotch.

It was easily the kinkiest swing I'd ever heard of.

I took the whip that was under my arm and clasped it between my legs while I slipped off the high heels. I pushed the spike of each heel into a chain link one on either side of me. This was going to be a bumpy ride and I'd need everything I could to hold onto.

"You may resume your original position." I ordered holding onto my shoe/hand holds.

I was lifted off the ground. I knew from my training that I could easily survive the fall if things went pear shaped, but that was only the logical part of my brain. The rest of me didn't want to look down.

"Are you a good girl or a slut, Lola?"

"I'm whatever you want me to be, Goddess."

"Then open your legs as wide as you can and show me what a good little slut you are."

"Yes, Goddess Rebecca."

She shifted one leg at a time until she was as wide open as she could possibly be and I could see everything. You didn't need to be Sherlock Holmes to tell she was getting off on her diminutive dominatrix.

Not gonna lie, all this sexy domme stuff was getting me going as well, but I couldn't let myself get distracted. I had a job to do and I was going to do it.

"This chain makes a perfect swing for a little Goddess like me."

I shifted my weight so she could feel me through the chains like a spider sensing a fly on her web. Only this fly was in control. Not large, but in charge.

"And it gives me a positively obscene view of your pussy. I like the fact that you haven't gone the full Brazilian route. I think a little hair down there is sexy. It reminds us that we're all just animals. Some more than others. Especially when it's matted down with your juices like it is now. And your lips. I can almost see them opening up to me like they were a flower and I was the Sun. Georgia O'Keefe must be rolling over in her wet dream at the thought."

I reached out with the whip and ran it over the small part of her breasts that I could reach.

"I'm about to make your dreams come true, Lola. I'm about to let you touch yourself while your Goddess watches you from her perch. Would you like that, pet?"

"Very much, my Goddess."

"But before I let you have your fun, tell me, are you a righty? Is that the hand you use to rub one out when you think about some nothing of a girl owning you?"

"yes"

"Today you're going to use your left hand. Do you know why?"

"Because my Goddess wishes it."

"Good answer." I switch hands and rub the whip along her other breast. "Just this once your Goddess will explain the mysterious ways she moves.

"I saw you fumbling around with those nipple clamps. How hard it was for you keeping your balance with just your weak left arm for support. I don't even want to think about what could have happened to me if I was perched on my swing while you were flailing around like that. And that was just putting on a pair of clamps. Who knows how crazy you'll get once you're three fingers into it. So you're gonna use your dominant hand to keep me from becoming a fallen Goddess. It won't feel as good for you diddling yourself with your off hand, but that's not the point. Do you know what the point is?"

Silence except for Lola's heavier and heavier breathing.

"It wasn't a rhetorical question, slave."

"Because my pleasure isn't as important as the safety and dignity of my Goddess."

"You're so full of good answers today I may even let you cum. We'll see. Now put your diddling hand in front of me and I'll give you my blessing."

I held on tight to my makeshift handholds as the giant boobs I was hanging from started to sway back and forth. Lola placed her left hand in front of me and awaited further orders. I stared at it for awhile letting Lola's anticipation bubble. Then I leaned forward and pressed my elbows into the pad of her dirty hands.

"You've just touched your Goddess' breasts." It was a blatant lie, but she wasn't going to know the difference and I wanted to save as much of me for Tina as I could. "What do you say?"

"Thank you, Goddess Rebecca."

"You have my blessing. You may masturbate."

Her left hand flew to her vulva before I'd finished the last syllable of my sentence.

There was no need for foreplay. Or maybe everything we had been doing since I walked through the hangar door was foreplay. Either way she was ready for this. She pressed two fingers past her wet lips and rubbed the tip of her thumb against her clit. I had to order her to shift her butt a couple times to give me a good viewing angle.

She was trying hard not to jostle her tiny Goddess, but it was impossible for her to keep her torso completely still while kneading herself like that. I held onto my shoes and wrapped my legs together behind the chain. It was gonna be one hell of a show, but it was gonna be a rough ride.

The experience did take me out of the domme headspace I'd worked myself into. It was impossible to feel that powerful and confident when you saw what I saw from where I saw it. I could try to remind myself that I was the one steering this ship, but you don't feel like the Captain when you're dangling from a chain in the engine room.

I watched fingers as large as I was massaged and entered desperate lips that were wider than most doors. Aroused heat radiated down from a heart the size of a submarine engine. More heat and the scent of her burning need wafted outwards from her crotch.

Every new wave of her pleasure caused her body to shift ever so slightly. She barely noticed it, but when the motion reached her breasts I found myself swinging like a chandelier in a Zorro movie.

It's hard to feel in control, or even adequate, when you're in the middle of that.

It brought home the weeks of forced purity. At that moment I wanted nothing more than to interact with Lola … Jordan like a real person. At the same level and size. To satisfy our mutual want and make her stop feeling ashamed about her sexuality. Then curl up in each other's arms. Spent and happy.

I didn't even notice that my hand had wandered down to my crotch until I started pushing the bathing suit aside. I thought about Tina and felt so damned guilty for cheating on her like this. Getting off to another woman while she was probably worried sick about me. Wondering where I was. Crying over pictures of me.

CRACK!

The whip was just long enough to reach Lola's masturbating hand. Her whole body trembled at the hit, but she kept the damage to me to a minimum.

"Slow down, slave. I want to savor this."

"Yes, my Goddess." her voice was just lust pushed out of her lungs.

I felt bad whipping her just cause I was feeling guilty. I tried to convince myself that the full force of my tiny whip only amounted to a nasty bug bite to a giant like her. I tried to tell myself that subs don't feel pain like normal people do. But I knew I needed to take control of myself and the easiest way to do that was to take back control of Lola.

"This is what we're going to do. I'm going to start swinging on my little tit trapeze here and you're going to match the pace I set. Like a metronome only a whole lot more fun."

Lola grunted her understanding.

It took me a minute to shift the momentum of just bouncing around with Lola's boobs into an independent swing. I thought Lola was going to explode, and not in the way she wanted, waiting for me to get moving. It definitely meant that I had to keep both hands on the shoes with the whip tucked under my butt. At least it kept my cheating hands from wandering.

"Tell me when you're close, slave. If you cum without permission I will crawl inside your vag and personally cover every millimeter of it with tabasco and sand."

"yes"

I worked the pace up slowly. Teasing her with her own

obedience. I stared in awe at her raw display of sexuality. Her world had become the sensation between her legs driven to the beat of of my weight tugging on her abused nipples swinging back and forth like a hypnotist's pocket watch.

"I am so rubbing one out when I'm done here." I said under my breath. Lola was too far gone to hear me anyway.

"I'm getting close, Goddess." She was having trouble speaking.

"You need to ask me fore permission before I let you cum, slave."

"May I cum, Goddess Rebecca? Pretty please."

"Not like that."

"How?" That one syllable expressed more longing than a Faulkner novel.

"How do mortals petition their Goddesses?"

It took her a moment. "They pray?"

"You'e already on you knees."

Lola didn't say anything for what seemed like a very long time. I was starting to worry that I'd touched on a hard limit that Maria didn't know about. I was about to pull my whip out from under my ass to motivate her when she started.

"My Goddess, who art between my breasts, hallowed be thy name. Thy will be done, my pussy cum, for Lola as it is for Rebecca."

"Cum, slave."

The spasm started between her legs and exploded up her spine. Her bucking body threw me from my perch despite her best intentions. I managed to grab hold of the chain before I fell too far, but the whip was now laying if a leather puddle on the floor. I wrapped the chain around me as best I could and rode out the orgasm storm.

She screamed something, but I was too busy holding onto the chain for it to register in the moment. It was only afterwards that I could tell she was shouting out my name.

"That was … wow." I said after the last of the major tremors had passed.

I let myself drop to the floor, but kept my eyes glued to Lola's still quivering sex and the wet hand that rested at its entrance.

"Pry your labia apart with your fingers. I want to see inside of you, Lola."

Lola said something I didn't pay attention to and obeyed.

It was the most beautiful thing I had ever seen. Slick and smooth. Perfectly pink and still trembling. I wanted to crawl inside until there was no part of me that wasn't engulfed in her. I wanted to crawl to her center and kiss her from the inside.

Most of all I wanted her to be Tina.

"You can close them now. I'm done."

I walked out from under Lola still head tripping from what I'd just been through.

I took my time putting the whip away. I needed the few extra seconds to clear my head so I could finish this scene.

"I liked your prayer, Lola."

"Thank you, Goddess Rebecca."

"And I liked the show you put on for me. I think you deserve an extra special reward for that."

Lola's eyes saucered.

"Is that your water bowl over there?" I already knew the answer.

"Yes. The gardner, Bertie, he fills it up for me every morning when he feeds me."

"There's still a lot there."

"It's still early, Goddess. I need to ration it or I get so thirsty at night."

"I think I'll bathe in it for you."

"What?" She hadn't expected that.

"I am going to strip myself naked and wash myself in your only source of drinking water. Then every time you take a drink you will taste me. Do you think that's a suitable reward for the obedience you have displayed here today?"

"If you wish it, Goddess."

"That's not good enough, slave. You have to want it. I know you say you're straight. That the idea of being topped by a woman is humiliating for you. You have to convince me that you want to drink my bath water. You have to beg me for it."

I stood near the water bowl and listened to her pleas for degradation. After a few minutes of listening to her pathetically beg for something she didn't want I stopped her.

"I hear your prayers, slave. I'll bathe in your bowl."

Lola looked relieved.

"There's just one catch. I'm a deity. I can't have you turning into a pillar of salt or a deer cause you see something mortals aren't supposed to gaze upon. And let's face it, seeing your Goddess in her altogether is top of that list. So you're going to have to close your eyes while I'm taking my bath."

"Yes, Goddess Rebecca." She sounded as disappointed as a six year old who got socks for Christmas.

She closed her eyes.

I ran my hands along side the dog bowl. It was taller than me, but not by much. Like an above ground jacuzzi. I wiggled out of my suit and hung it over the edge of the dish. I was just tall enough and strong enough to pull myself up on the lip of the bowl and drop inside.

The water was warmer than I'd thought, but I wasn't there to get clean.

I splashed around very loudly for several minutes letting Lola's imagination kick into overdrive. The thought of her fantasizing about me was a little stimulating, but I was mostly focused on what I had to do.

"Seeing you rub one out like that really inspired me, Lola. And this water feels so good against my naked skin. You wouldn't mind if I played with myself right here? In your drinking water?"

"My Goddess can do whatever she wants." She sounded humble with an edge of anxiety in her voice.

"I get so wet when I play with myself. Especially when I'm as horny as I am right now. It would be like you were drinking straight from my pussy." I splashed some more water. "Would you like that?"

"yes"

"I thought you would."

I didn't say anything else. I just made sure that I was loud enough for Lola to hear everything I did. When I was done I pulled myself wet and dripping from the bowl and placed my still dry swimsuit on the hand Lola had masturbated with.

I pulled on the cloak before telling her she could open her eyes. When she did, she was disappointed to not see me nude.

"You can take the clamps off your nipples in an hour." I said.

"But I don't have a clock, Goddess Rebecca."

"Then guess. But guess right cause if you take them off any earlier you are in so much trouble." And I walked out of the hangar.

"That was incredible." Maria hadn't even waited for me to step off the elevator before she started talking at me. "How did you do that?"

"I'm a theater minor with a history of very kinky ex-girlfriends." I said walking over my tiny table and collapsing into my little chair. "Were you watching me … us?"

"Yes. And you really made Jordan's fantasy come true. I honestly didn't think you had it in you, but you were one hell of a little dominatrix."

"Being a domme is mostly putting on a show for an audience of one. Two if the giant who owns you is a voyeur." I gave Maria the stink eye.

"We have to monitor Jordan for her own safety. Sight. Sound. There are even sensors in the walls that keep track of her vitals. Trust me, you really pushed her buttons. Especially when you … you know … in her water dish."

"I totally faked that."

"Really?" Maria sounded skeptical.

"It's bad enough I'm topping someone behind Tina's back, I'm not going to rub one out for them. It's bad enough I had to watch her get off, but you said it was one of her favorite fantasies."

"So why even pretend?"

"A magician never reveals her secrets, but give me some wine and I'll Penn and Teller it for you."

Maria didn't look like she was happy with my suggestion.

"Please."

I begged with my puppy dog eyes. I needed a drink so bad after what I'd just done. And some pants. I hadn't stopped by my room to get properly dressed before coming up. I knew where I could find clothes, but only Maria could give me access to vino.

Maria left. When she came back she had a me-sized coffee cup filled with red wine. I held the cup between my fingers and took my first sip.

"You were about to reveal what's behind the curtain." Maria said after my third sip.

"Sorry. After a scene like that it can take me awhile to process everything.

"Jordan got off on me taking control, but she needed something more. Something that could stay with her when I'm not there. Getting her to think that I was infusing her water with my girl power gave her mind something fun to imagine. She was fantasizing about me doing it while I was in there. She'll probably go to sleep tonight still thinking about it."

"That's a safe bet."

"So." I placed my empty cup on the table. "I've given you what Jordan wants, how long before I get to see Tina again?"

"We'll see."

Seven: Walkies

Maria's "we'll see" turned out to be a lot longer than I'd thought it'd be when I first took Jordan for a spin. After a few days I was starting to bounce off the walls. After two weeks I was making escape plans.

Which wasn't so easy when you were living in an aquarium. An electronic one anyway. Maria had told me that Jordan was under surveillance. She slipped up a couple times over breakfast or lunch and said some things that made me think that my little apartment had been bugged too. Which was creepy. This whole place was creepy.

Still way better than Lauren.

Speaking of creepy, I found out what the deal was with Jordan's kennel. The entire thing is ringed with little hallways for me to walk through. Each lined with one way glass facing my mammoth slave girl. I can see everything she does, but all she sees is what looks like tile. The stairs I passed when I first explored led up to different levels so I could look at Jordan from any angle I wanted to and she would never know.

Maria says Jordan thought of the idea herself.

Every day went pretty much the same as the last. I'd wake up in my incredible bed, get ready for my day, breakfast with Maria, then go downstairs so Jordan could be topped by a tiny. Sometimes I'd "make" Jordan have an orgasm. Sometimes I just left her wanting. A feeling I was experiencing a lot of after I discovered that I'd been bugged. At least I had that one magical night with the bathtub faucet before I realized I had an audience.

Aside from the keeping me there against my will aspects of our relationship Maria seemed nice. She wasn't a bad person, she just cared about Jordan a hell of a lot more than she did about me. Jordan gave up everything for her except her kink. I was just some freak who signed away my size.

I didn't really get to know Jordan despite our time together. A dominatrix sees a part of a sub that is very true, but not very them. Like that analogy of the blind men describing an elephant. I got to touch a part of her that most people would never even know was there, but there was so much of her I'd never get to experience be-cause I couldn't get past the tail. Some nights I'd walk the hallways around her kennel and watch her kneeling there on the uncomfortable concrete. I tried to get inside her head, but my telepathy could only pick up the kinky shit I'd make her do the next day.

Then I started feeling guilty about spying on her so I stopped.

After two weeks I was running out of things to make her do to herself or ways to insert myself into her kinks. Okay. Maybe I should have used a word other than "insert." That didn't happen. I never touched her lady junk and she never touched mine. Jordan never even saw me naked. I was already semi-cheating on Tina, I wasn't about to find out what a tongue the size of a sofa cushion would feel like between my legs.

Not that Jordan didn't offer.

You know, in that passive-aggressive way that subs have.

I was talking with Maria one morning about running out of ideas for scenes when she suggested my escape plan for me.

"Why don't you take her out on the grounds?" Maria said over coffee.

"Like she's a dog? Not that I haven't treated her that way already, just clarifying."

"I think she'd like that. And the idea of being outside buck nekkid while you put her through her paces. You both could probably use the fresh air and it'd give Bertie a chance to properly clean her kennel."

"Do you think I could get some low strength nipple clamps. I've got an idea for something, but regular ones might cause permanent damage."

"I'm sure I can find something. Care to tell me what you have in mind?"

"You'll see."

"You know what you're doing. Apparently. I'll talk to Bertie about scheduling this tomorrow. I'll have him add the clamps to the equipment rack when he feeds Jordan. They'll be marked in red so you know you haven't grabbed the wrong pair."

"I'll need a couple other things."

"What?"

"Grab a shopping list."

Jordan was sleeping when I walked into her kennel that morning.

There wasn't much room for her to get comfortable so she just curled up with her head pillowed on her arms and her butt haunched in the air. She looked so sweet and pure with her eyes closed I hated waking her, but Bertie was waiting and I needed to start my escape. I'd need Jordan for that.

I'm not going to lie. As escape plans went this wasn't exactly the best thought out or organized one in the history of hijinks. But there's not much you can do when you look up to Thumbelina and your hench-woman's naked, under constant surveillance, and has a huge lady boner to be your slave girl. In my defense my track record for life changing decisions hadn't exactly been the greatest over the past my entire life.

My plan hinged on Bertie. He probably wasn't as nice as he seemed, but that's only because nobody could be as nice as he seemed. He was like what you're kind Uncle Phil was supposed to be like. Only if Uncle Phil came out of central casting for a version of Lady Chatterly's Lover where the casting director didn't really read the book and was just going the type of hot earthy guy all the straight girls swooned over. He was painfully embarrassed to be around his former boss while she exploring her sexuality with a Lilliputian dominatrix. He was always sweet and polite to the two of us, but you could tell he just wanted to get the duck out of Fodge when he had to deal with us directly.

Bertie'd be busy cleaning the kennel while Jordan and I made our escape. And he probably wouldn't be too quick to run after us once he'd finished since that would mean seeing us cavorting in the grown up way that made him blush like a school girl. Which was good since he knew the grounds better than either of us and could probably run faster than a barefoot ex-heiress.

That left Maria and the household staff to worry about. I was pretty sure that Maria wasn't that interested in seeing me put her form-er boss through her paces. Sure she'd watch for the first few minutes to make sure Jordan was enjoying herself, but she'd find something better to do after she was sure Jordan was getting her submissive jollies.

Maria had made it clear to me that only Bertie, her, and I knew about what Jordan was doing. As far as the staff was concerned the former lady of the house was away on a vacation to someplace sunny getting lotion rubbed into her skin by sexy natives. I was pretty sure that Maria would do whatever it took to keep the maids from seeing their former boss prancing around naked on all fours on the lawn. They'd get the day off or be put on some long project on the other side of the house. Or something. I didn't need to know those details.

I figured there would be some kind of electronic surveillance, but it's not like Maria could have the entire outdoors bugged. I'm sure we'd reach the end of the line at some point and she'd send Bertie out to fetch us. I'd just have to make sure that we got to where we needed to be before he could get there.

I had a vague idea of how big the grounds were. There was only so much I could ask without making everyone suspicious. I didn't even feel safe asking Jordan. Too many bugs listening in. But once we were outside I could get better directions to a road or the neighbor's property. All we'd have to do would be to get off the grounds and get someone's attention. Once we had that we could get them to call Tina. OK, Tina's lawyer. McCaskill would get me out of here if it meant tearing the place down brick by brick.

Yeah, the plan was holier than swiss cheese, but it was all I had and I needed to do something. I needed to see Tina.

I walked over to the sleeping Jordan and tapped her nose with my leather boot. She blinked awake staring at me. She seemed confused at first then I remembered what I was wearing and chalked it up to that. It's not every morning that you get woken up by a tiny woman in full cowgirl cosplay. It wasn't the sexiest outfit I'd worn. Although I was rocking those jeans. But it was both thematically appropriate and practical. And did I mention the jeans? Cause there's been a lot said about my boobs, but I'm fun to watch coming or going.

"Time to wake up, Lola. We're going outside."

"Goddess?"

"OPEN UP!" I yelled at the door to real world.

The huge metal door flew open. The ground beneath me rumbled at the movement. Well, at least I could feel it. I'm pretty sure Jordan didn't notice anything.

A wave of fresh air and sunlight washed in. For the first time since I'd been shrunk I was breathing air that hadn't been circulated through an air conditioner and feeling naked sunlight on my face.

"That feels amazing." I said, closing my eyes and opening my arms to the outdoors.

"Good morning, Ms. Hogarth." Bertie said. I could make out his impossibly large silhouette against the light. "What will you be wanting today?"

"I've decided to take Lola out for a ride. Could you do me a solid and saddle her for me? I'm a little too … you know … small."

"Of course, Ms. Hogarth."

My saddle was hanging on the implement rack facing Jordan. It had been there since Maria filled my shopping list. Dangling there mysteriously, making Jordan wonder exactly what I was going to do with it. Fantasizing about how I was going to ride her. What part of her body I was going to mount.

Bertie got down on his knees closer to Jordan's level, but still towering above her thanks to the extra headroom in the doorway. He pulled a leather collar out of his jacket pocket and worked it around Jordan's neck. He was very careful about where his hands and his eyes went. The early morning light caught both of their blushes.

After some adjustments Bertie was satisfied that the collar was in place and secure. He reached over to the wall and carefully lifted up my saddle between his giant thumb and forefinger. It took him four tries to attach saddle to collar, but when he was done it wasn't going to come off without a giant doing the removing.

I walked over to the wall and found the nipple clamps marked in red. I slung them over my shoulder and sauntered over to my giant nervous steed.

"What's happening, Goddess?" Jordan sounded nervous. I don't know how much of that was from Bertie or how much of it was from the open door and the threat of going outside.

"You're smarter than that, Lola. What do you think is happening?"

Jordan just knelt their silently.

I walked over to her forearm and climbed my way up onto her shoulder. I carefully balanced and made my way to the saddle. I gingerly lowered myself onto the hard leather then draped the clamps down on either side of her neck. Bertie reached down and placed a clamp on each of Jordan's earlobes.

"Thanks, Bertie." I said.

"No problem." The giant replied.

"Alright, Lola." I turned my attention back to Jordan. "I'm sure you used to go horseback riding before you were my pet. So I'm pretty sure you know the way this is gonna work. I tug on your left ear I want you to go left. I tug on you right, I want you to go right. I want you to go faster, I'll dig my spurs into your flanks. You stay on all fours unless I tell you otherwise. Got it?"

"Yes, Goddess."

"That's my girl." I said, digging my spurs into her neck and giving the reins a snap.

The giant slave girl lurched forward almost sending me crashing off my tiny saddle. I grabbed on tighter and let her crawl out into the sun.

It was freaky.

And I'm not just talking about the fact that I was riding the world's sexiest Thanksgiving float. That was weird, but the sort of weird I'd acclimated to. Over the past few weeks I'd gotten used to a lot of things that literally made me pee myself when I first shrank. People the size of King Kong. Rooms bigger than most office buildings. I had managed to cope with them.

What I hadn't wrapped my brain around was how big the outside world really was to me. I saw trees larger than the Sears Tower looming over me filled with birds that may as well have been astronauts they were so far off the ground. And a sky that went on forever.

I let Jordan keep on walking forward while I had my little melt down. Every once in awhile I'd pull her in a random direction so she'd think I was still in control. I was terrified out of my tiny mind, but I couldn't let Jordan see that. Jordan needed a powerful dominant woman to obey; not some frightened little mouse. And I needed Jordan to get my ass out of this mess.

I pulled my eyes away from the terrible sky and just stared at the back of Jordan's neck. The flesh I was riding on was something I knew. Something I could wrap my head around. It was still a little alien to me, but it was the sort of alien weird I could handle.

"Lola." I said, slowly to make sure she couldn't hear my fear. "Where is the nearest road?"

"There's the driveway out front."

The saddle I was clinging to for dear life to was attached to a collar around Jordan's throat. When she spoke the words vibrated through my entire body. I hadn't expected that. The sensation was unnerving and a little bit sexy, but at least it gave me something more to think about than the God Trees we were now walking under.

"No. I mean the nearest road. You know, with traffic. And people."

"Why do you want to know?"

I could feel every word beat against my body. Especially the fun parts of me that were crammed against the saddle. Parts of me that wanted her to keep on talking until I was a wet spent mess. I didn't need that. I needed to be sharp and focused and all Cool Hand Luke. Not some desperate woman who couldn't think straight when she got a little horny.

"Because you are talking back to your owner, Lola. Because you are questioning me. I think you need to be punished. I think I need to show everybody what you really are. Don't you? Let them see how far you've fallen. Let them see you crawling on your hands and knees naked while a little woman rides you like the dumb animal you really are. Now start moving or I'll let them pet you too."

"Yes, Goddess."

The vibrating words reminded me how long it had been since I'd had any fun. It took all my willpower not to order Jordan to just recite the Pledge of Allegiance, or the Gettysburg Address, or just keep on saying nonsense words until I got some relief.

The important thing was she was moving. Pretty quickly for someone crawling.

We would have been able to make it faster if I'd had Jordan stand up and walk on her hind legs, but I had no idea how far Maria's electronic eyes reached. She might already be suspicious of us going out past a certain point. If Jordan suddenly got to her feet and started running she'd call out the proverbial dogs.

Things got better for me once we were under more tree cover. Everything still seemed vastly enormous to me, but at least now there was a feeling of enclosed space. Like the tree limbs were just a really odd ceiling.

My fear wasn't completely gone, but it was better. I distracted myself from it and my sexy thoughts by running through the speech I was going to give to whoever found us. I'd been practicing it since I came up with this plan and I have to say I was pretty damn convincing.

That's when I first heard the buzzing sound.

At first I thought it was some bugs. Maybe a beehive somewhere in the distance. I'd never liked bugs when I was normal. The thought of having to deal with a bee bigger than my head was truly traumatic.

I spurred Jordan to go faster.

We'd been going another five minutes and the buzzing wasn't getting any quieter. But it wasn't getting any louder either. I forced my eyes away from Jordan's neck and started scanning the trees for whatever it was that was following us. I missed it at first, but finally noticed it flying around behind us floating just a couple feet below the tree branches.

A drone.

"Sugar honey ice tea."

It was obviously following us. And it probably had a camera. And GPS. Maria knew exactly where we were and what we were doing. Headed towards the road and out of Maria's life. Was there any sort of lie I could come up with to cover this? If there was it was being too damn quiet for its own good. Bertie was probably already running this way ready to take us back to the house.

Jordan was going to be OK, she was Maria's friend and benefactor after all. There was no way she was going to be any worse off than she was already. And let's face it, if things did get worse for her she'd probably like it.

I, on the other foot, was a totally different matter. Technically I was property. Property who tried to kidnap the friend and would be sex slave of a very wealthy former maid. Things were not going to go that well for me. Best case scenario I never got to see Tina again. Worst … well, Maria didn't seem like the murdering type, but in my case it wouldn't be murder. I don't think even PETA gave a fuck about me.

"Jordan." I said, using her real name for the first time in forever. "I need you to get on your feet and run to the road. Do it! Now!"

I pushed my forearms into the gap between the collar and Jordan's neck. There wasn't time for her to pick me up and run so I'd just have to hang on as best I could. I felt the world shift out from under me as the ground beneath my feet transformed into a wall that I was barely able to cling to.

Jordan moved with the lightning speed of the giants turning everything around me into a blur of greens and browns. I couldn't make out the drone anymore, but I could still hear it. By the sound of it the drone was having no problem keeping up with us.

I kicked Jordan trying to urge her to go faster, but I doubt if she even felt my tiny feet bounce off her thick skin. I yelled out her name, but my little words were drowned out by the rush of wind from her speeding body.

Jordan was breathing hard and each breath tightened the collar a little bit more. My arms felt like they were about to be cut off from the increased pressure as they were pushed harder and harder into the giant's hot sweaty skin. Whatever was keeping my saddle attached to the collar snapped. Loudly. I watched it spin off and disappear into the swirl of chaos behind us.

I could still hear the drone just as close as it had been.

The pressure on my forearms was getting worse and worse with each lungful of air Jordan gulped down. I swear I could feel her pulse reverberating through the leather, getting faster and stronger the more she ran. I had this image in my head of those old school thermometers. The ones with mercury in them that you only see at your grandma's or equally ancient cartoons. I had this cartoon memory of someone putting a lighter up to one of them and watching the mercury explode out the top.

That's what my hands felt like.

I needed to get my arms out of there while I still had arms. I was a little vague on how I'd hold on to the running behemoth who sorta shared a name with the woman I loved, but that wasn't as important as not becoming the world's first shrunken double amputee. I'd burn that bridge when I came to it.

I pulled myself up as far as I could then stretched my legs up even further. I must have looked pretty damn stupid squatting there attached to Jordan's neck, my shoulders slouched down because of my trapped arms and my feet almost level with my neck as I rested the bottoms of my boots on the top of Jordan's collar. Thank you, Carly for making me take that yoga class with you.

The buzzing of the drone was still coming up fast behind us.

I pushed down on the rigid leather with all the strength my legs could muster. I could feel my arms begin to slip free. Every other step there was a split second when the collar would loosen a fraction of a hair. It wasn't much, but neither was I. Our combined sweat gave us some lubrication, but rubbing the hot salt water on raw skin just traded one pain for another.

My hands felt like throbbing boils, but I managed to slowly work them out of the trap I'd stuck them in. Every other step saw me a little closer to freedom and comfort. Even though I could still hear the drone behind us I was feeling pretty optimistic. We still had a pretty good lead on Bertie. All we had to do was not cut off my arms, make it to the road, and I'd be with Tina. Where I belonged.

That's about the time the poop hit the fan.

It's hard to say exactly what happened. Maybe Jordan tripped on a root. Maybe the drone did something to her. With everything moving so fast it was all a blur to me. The only thing I can say for certain was I went from getting my arms the last couple of hand lengths out of the collar to laying flat on my back on the ground woozily looking up at the giant woman crouched on the ground above me.

I was too dazed to even realize it was Jordan until she pulled herself to her feet and started running away.

Without me.

"Nononononono." I wanted to scream, but there wasn't enough breath left in my little body.

I staggered to my feet still dizzy from the fall and aching from the landing. I stumbled forward pushing myself in Jordan's direction, but her giant legs had already carried her almost out of sight. I tried to run after her. OK. I know how stupid that sounds given how tiny I am and how huge she is, but I was scared and probably a little concussed.

I didn't make it that far.

Part of it was me. I was a mess. Most of the rest of it was the undergrowth I was neck deep in. Jordan had no problem stomping her giant naked feet through it, but I ended up getting my cowgirl shirt stuck on a twig the size of a branch and my spurs got stuck in a blade of grass taller than I was. I tried harder, but all I managed to do was get myself dug in deeper.

I felt like crying when I saw Jordan's bare butt disappear from view. I felt an almost overwhelming urge to just go fetal and bawl my eyes out, but I knew I'd wind up dead if I did.

Then I heard the drone.

I must have been hearing it all along. It's not like it had some sort of stealth mode it could turn on and off. I must have just been too numb to recognize it for what it was. Now that I was no longer being dragged around the forest strapped down to Jordan's neck I could clearly see it hovering over head.

I'd risked a lot to get away from it, but now that I was separated from Jordan, alone in a giant nightmare forest, and epically failing at trailblazing, the thought of Maria's punishment didn't seem all that bad. At least Maria was a person I could reason with. A hungry snake or owl wasn't going to give me that option.

"Take me to your leader." I called up to the drone. My hands were up in the air in the surrender pose I'd learned from watching way too many bad movies.

I watched as the drone hovered directly over me. Would it just hang in the air giving Bertie a buzzing landmark … airmark? … to find me? Or would it just swing down low and expect me to climb on? Maybe it had some sort of suction dart/rope thing it was going to shoot me with. I wasn't really loving that last one, but little shrunk ladies in the woods can't be chosers.

The drone didn't get any lower. It probably couldn't land on the rough ground. When no secret compartment opened up to rubber dart me I resigned myself to being picked up by Bertie when he finally got here.

That hope lasted until the drone flew off in the direction Jordan had run.

"NO!" I waved my arms frantically over my head. "I'm giving up. This means I'm giving up."

I tried to run again, but all I managed was to trip in the ginormous grass. As I fell I heard my cowgirl shirt rip on the twig branch I was already half impaled on. It kept me from falling, but I was dangling from it my feet no longer touching the ground.

"Stop. PLEASE." I thrashed my arms and legs helplessly in the air as I watched my only hope fly away. "You can't leave me here, I'll die."

Eight: Abandoned

"Fuckity fuck fuck fuck."

The buzz of the drone was long gone by the time I finally ripped myself off my twig perch. Which would have been great if my spurs weren't still stuck in the grass above my head. Now I was dangling from my feet like some yuppie in a pair of very badly placed gravity boots alternating between feeling sorry for myself and being pissed at Maria for abandoning me.

"I sooo should have listened to you, Carly."

The blood was rushing to my head and I didn't know if that was a good thing or a bad one. I wasn't feeling as woozy as I was before, but that might not be a good thing. I tried to pull myself up to undue the spurs, but that wasn't happening. Yoga had made me bendier then a lot of other women, but there was no way I was pulling off a vertical sit up.

I kept pulling my feet down. The plan was to pull the spurs out, but I ended up pulling my feet out of the boots instead.

"OK. That works too."

I lay there on the rough ground looking up at my fake cowboy boots dangling from a blade of grass that was taller than I was. I looked down and did a damage assessment of my shirt. It didn't take long. What I had left was literally a pair of sleeves connected by a few threads. I looked like I'd survived some sort of sexy apocalypse. OK, a PG-13 sexy apocalypse; my bra was intact and keeping me from an R rating.

Maybe it was the concussion I thought I got a while back. Maybe it was all the blood that rushed to my head when I was dangling from the grass. But I imagined myself ditching the ripped up shirt, leaving the boots in the grass, losing the jeans and the chaps, and running around like some 50's jungle queen from a pre-code comic.

Which was stupid.

"I'm not even wearing leopard print undies."

Resigned to stay dressed, I got to my feet. I felt steadier than I had before. That was good. I wasn't exactly loving walking on dirt in my stocking feet, but it could have been worse. I reached for my boots, but they were too high now that my weight wasn't bending the stalk down.

I grabbed the stalk of grass and let my weight drag it down until my boots were dangling at face level. I held the stalk with one hand and reached out to grab my boots with the other. They still wouldn't come loose so I put both hands on them and yanked. Hard. My hands slipped and the stalk sprang back upright taking my boots with it.

With enough force to free the trapped spurs and catapult my boots out of sight.

"You have got to be kidding me." I bent the stalk back expecting to see my boots still there. They weren't. "Grass doesn't even work like that."

I let the stalk go.

I took a deep breath and counted to ten.

"OK. Focus on the positives, Becks." I said to myself. "The headache is gone. Walking is easier now that you're head's clear. I'm lost in the woods on a millionaire's estate, which may as well be the size of Vermont cause I'm shrunk smaller than balls in the Arctic, but I'm not freaking out. Not me. No sir. Which probably means I'm in shock. And when the shock wears off I'll just go fetal until I die of exposure or get eaten by a colony of poisonous ants.

I took another breath.

"I am not going to accept that. That's just the sort of defeatist thinking that gets people killed out here. I am in a turd burger of a situation, but there's still a lot I can do. I just need to stay calm and figure out what that is."

I made my way through the underbrush. I didn't really have any plan or direction in mind. Mostly I needed to do something to keep from melting down. And to prove to myself that I could at least get around out here. It wasn't easy. I'd have traded my right arm for a machete. But it was manageable.

It wasn't long before I found myself in a very small clearing. Like barely big enough for me to fit in, it was so small. It took me a few seconds to pick up on the fact that I'd wandered into one of Jordan's foot prints. She was running pretty hard when she made it. Probably didn't even have time for all of her foot to hit the ground before she was pulling it up again.

And there was blood.

Of course there was blood. She was more of an indoor gal than I was and I made her run through the woods barefoot and naked. Of course she was going to get cut. I felt shitty for what I'd put her through. Then I felt even shittier for not thinking about it until now.

Maybe I deserved being left here to die.

"Now. If I were an outdoorsy person, what would I do first?" Talking always made me feel better, even if I was the only one there to hear me.

I'd get out of the outdoors, Rebecca.

"Great point, Becks, but not exactly helpful."

How about this for a point? People who start having heartfelt conversations with themselves two minutes after getting lost in the woods are a billion time more likely to get eaten by a squirrel.

"Touche, me."

I stopped talking and started moving. I probably would have done both, but getting through the underbrush, while manageable, still wasn't easy. I was sparing my voice for a stream of profanity and whining that I'll elect to not share.

All-in-all I think I got up to a whopping snail miles per hour.

I decided that I needed to find Jordan. I got her into this mess and I was still feeling pretty damn guilty about it. Even if it was delayed guilt. Besides, if I found her she could rescue me. Or we could both wait for Bertie or Maria to rescue both of us and deal with the consequences of my botched escape later.

And it was something I could do. I had no idea which way the mansion was. Or how far it was to the road. Or if the road was exactly in the direction I thought it was.

But I didn't need to be a Girl Scout to follow Jordan; Godzilla left a subtler trail through Tokyo.

So I pushed on through the thick grass and bramble that lay under the tree line. I still had trouble looking up. The world just seemed more intense and terrifying once I saw my place in it and nothing put me in my place as fast as a tree the size of the Chrysler Building.

I took short rests in Jordan's foot prints. When I could I'd climb a fallen branch or up a dandelion to get a view of the path ahead. I couldn't really see that far ahead thanks to the trees, but it did make things easier.

I had no idea how long I had been going. I couldn't tell time by the sun back when I was normal and looking up didn't freak me out so much. All I knew was that I was going forever and didn't feel any closer than when I'd started. I was running on empty, scared of what would happen to me if I didn't find Jordan, and feeling defeated in every way a person could be defeated.

I was standing on the summit of a very small sapling when I saw the drone. On the ground. Crashed. With an arrow through it and no sign of Jordan other than a trail of her giant footprints running out of sight.

"Have I already said 'fuckity fuck fuck fuck?'"

My tiny legs were getting pretty tired by that point so it took me a while to push my way through the underbrush and make it to the wreckage. I'm not even sure why I bothered. It wasn't like I was going to fix the damn thing and fly it out of here. I knew enough about electronics to program my DVR and make toast. End of list. And it wasn't like it had a black box for me to scour for clues. Not that I'd need to. It was super obvious why it crashed.

The giant honking ass arrow going straight through it.

Maybe I just needed to touch it. To make it feel real so I could process the latest in a long string of WTFs my life had turned into.

The sides of the drone were cool to the touch. Did that mean it was shot down a while ago and had time to cool down? Maybe drones just ran cool and the shooter was still nearby. I was clueless; I'd never owned a drone.

I climbed up onto the main … deck … body … whatever. It felt slick beneath my stocking feet, but I managed to find my balance and make my way to the arrow sticking out from the other side.

It sure looked real.

I had to lay flat on my belly to reach down and touch the shaft. It wasn't wood and it didn't feel exactly like metal. Whatever it was it hadn't even been scratched punching its way through the drone's tough hull. The arrow head still looked razor sharp to me, but I wasn't about to shimmy out on the shaft to find out. I tried to close my hand around the pole-like shaft, but it was too big so I settled for making a rough measurement with my hand.

I imagined myself back on the ground trying to find my way back climbing a twig to get my bearings. Imaginary me heard a whoosh of air then looked down to see a thick almost metal pole sticking out of my chest. My imaginary eyes followed a trail of red up the pole to my still beating heart dangling like a flesh pinata from the razor sharp head.

I suddenly felt very vulnerable laying so far above the sheltering ground.

I scrambled off the drone as fast as I could. Sure it wasn't very likely to happen and it wasn't very rational, but I didn't feel safe again until I was crouching back down in the giant grass.

"So what's this guy doing playing Robin Cupid in the middle of the woods?"

Duh!

"OK. He's a hunter, obs. And he shot down the drone which means he doesn't want to get caught which means he's an illegal hunter which makes him a … what's the word?"

Poached.

"Or a serial killer who's gone all The Most Dangerous Game on us."

You need to make sure Jordan's OK.

"Shut up, Jiminy."

You're the reason she's out here. Alone. Naked. Terrified. Miles from safety. In the hands of some lunatic with a longbow.

"OK. OK. Shut up already. I'm moving. Jesum Crow, who knew I could be such a nag."

I kept my head down as I followed Jordan's trail. My freaked out paranoid side was convinced that a giant sniper was going to pop up and impale my tiny butt the second I popped my head up, but my saner side (yeah, I have one of those) mostly kept that in check.

I don't know exactly how long I spent crawling from one footprint to another, but my tummy was telling me I'd missed lunch. I was going to need to eat eventually, I just had no idea what I'd have. I'd spotted some berries from time to time, but they didn't look like any of the three berries I knew were safe to eat so I took a pass. I wasn't sure how much longer I could afford to be careful.

I came to the end of Jordan's trail after my third massive hunger pang.

The first thing I noticed was the stench. It smelt like someone had filtered skunk farts through vintage boiled pee. Even as low to the ground as I was my little eyes were watering up and it just got worse the closer I got. It was more than enough to put me off my appetite. Which may have been the shittiest silver lining in the history of grey clouds.

I made my way through the stank to a clearing that I guessed was part of Jordan's trail. Unlike the footprints I'd wandered into this was a pretty large area. Several times as big as I was if I had to guess and I had to guess cause my eyes were squinted shut so far from the skunk fart pee aroma that I was almost blind. I was mapping the clearing out on my hands and knees as blind as Velma without her glasses when my hand splashed into something warm, wet, and a little tacky.

"Don't be poop. Don't be poop. Don't be poop." I mantra-ed working up the guts to look at what was dripping off my hand.

I opened my eyes and saw red.

Once I could see it I swear I could taste the copper through the pores of the skin of my hand. It was definitely blood. Probably

Jordan's. And there was a pool of it wider than me cooling under me.

I ran back to the grass Lady Machbething the blood off my hands to what was left of my shirt. The knees of my chaps were still wet with it.

You have to find her.

"Can you just let me freak out in peace? Chill. Bertie will find her."

He could be hours away.

"Or five minutes. Besides, he's all Ranger Rick. He can track her."

The psycho with the bow is hiding his tracks. That's probably why this place smells like day five of a weeklong skunk orgy – to throw off blood hounds.

"One. I'm pretty sure skunks don't smell like that when they're having sexy time. Two. If Bertie can't track her, how am I supposed to?"

You're smaller than him. You can see things down here that he'll miss up there. You have to.

"Then what? Beat the longbow hunter from Deliverance with my stunning repartee?"

Leave a trail Bertie can follow.

I hated being right. Having good ideas like that were just going to get me into super-sized trouble.

I circled Jordan's crash site. I was guessing it was where she crashed. The blood made me wonder how many arrows were sticking inside her when she fell. Was she even still alive? Was I risking it all for a corpse?

Anyway I circled Jordan's crash site looking for something to point me towards her. At least the stink got weaker the further I got from the center. I was almost out of eye shot of the site when I found the scuff marks in the ground. Under what looked like undisturbed leaves.

"Bingo."

OK. I had no idea what this new "bingo" was exactly, but it was suspicious/weird in a way that I hoped meant I'd found something important. I didn't know if Deep Woods Hawkeye left 'em, but I was feeling Occam's Razor burn. I went a bit further and found another one. And another one after that.

"Trail has been found. Yay team Becks! Now, how do I mark it?"

I looked down at my ripped shirt, battered jeans, bloody chaps, and filthy socks.

"A world of 'no.'"

You don't have anything else.

"So I just get nakeder and nakeder the closer I get to some psycho auditioning for the Stallone roll in First Blood?"

Jordan needs you.

"This better be burning off some serious karma." I ripped the left sleeve off the rip that had previously been my shirt and threw it down on the ground.

You don't believe in karma.

"Shut up."

I left an piece of my ensemble at every fifth "bingo." My ripped up shirt was good for four pieces, but the chaps and jeans were too tough to rip apart with my bare hands. I was running out of strip poker chips way too fast. It wasn't long until I was down to my bra, panties, and socks.

"Look at me going all Sheena Queen of the Jungle. If Sheena traded in her fur bikini for a Victoria's Secret gift card. And wore socks."

I was halfway to the next bingo when I heard the buzzing. At first I thought Maria had sent out another drone, but the sound was different. Higher pitched. Faster. I risked looking up into the nightmare God sky, but didn't see anything but my own madness.

The sound kept getting closer.

I picked up the pace, but whatever the buzz was it followed me. There was something familiar about it. Maybe I'd have recognized it if I were normal, but my little ears weren't hearing it right.

The sound got louder. A lot louder. It spiked so bad I had to cover my ears to block out the railroad spikes being driven into my ears.

It didn't work.

Then I felt a hot wind brush against my almost naked back and exposed neck. I stopped dead in the archer's tracks when I felt something land on me. I felt several tiny hooked feet skitter on either side of my bra strap. Judging by how far apart they were I'd say whatever it was was a s big as my head, but I could barely feel its weight.

"What would Sheena do in a situation like this?" I was blathering, but I was at a point when all I had left was blather.

Stab it with her knife.

"I don't have one."

Feel free to freak out then.

I twisted my head back as far as I could. Cause I had to see whatever the eff had landed on me. But I turned wicked slow cause I really didn't want to see whatever the eff it was. My heart was beating so fast I was pretty sure it was about to cannon ball itself out of my chest. My adrenal gland was prepping the flight part of "fight or flight" when my eyes cleared my shoulder blade and I was staring it right in the kisser.

I'm going to call it a vampire. It's not what you'd call it, but that's what I'm going with. To me it was as big as a bat, flew through the air, and sucked blood. That's a vampire in my book. You'd call it a mosquito, but you never saw one the way I saw this bitch.

The vampire stared at me with a thousand faceted eyes as it clung to my back. It's monofang was already embedded in my back. I could see the red trail of my precious bodily fluids getting sucked up and out of my body where they belonged.

I hadn't even felt it.

The vampire sure as fuck felt it when I belted her. It was still tethered to me by the monofang so it was slow to react to my fist. It didn't have time to fly away before my pissed fist thundered down on its furry sack of an excuse for a body. In the vampire's defense even I didn't know I was gonna do that until I felt my punch connect. I was all reptile brain or caveman brain or whatever part of you makes you instinctively wail at something that's sucking the life out of you to feed its egs.

When I was normal I could squash mosquitos with the best of them. The best mini-me could do was knock this vampire bitch off me and maybe daze her a little.

"NYAAAHHHH!" I hadn't felt the fang go in, but I sure as heck felt it coming out.

I reached my hand around and felt for the wound between my shoulder blades. This time my hand came back wet with my own blood. Was I bleeding or had the vampire peed a little of my own blood back on me when I knocked her lights out? I was too busy staring at the stunned monster to find out.

She staggered on the ground woozy from my punch and drunk on my blood. I stood there with my fist out like an olde time-y boxer hoping that her 1,000 eyes couldn't see through my fake courage. It seemed like I was standing there for hours waiving my fists out in front of me, but it was probably only a minute before the vampire went off into the deepening shadows, fazed, but still flying.

There may have been a little meltdown on my part at that moment.

I was pretty sure I wasn't bleeding. At least blood stopped coming off on my hands after the next couple of wipes. I had no idea where that mosquito had been or what it was carrying, but I was pretty sure I was going to get something painful and deadly from the bite. And I probably deserved it after what I'd done to Jordan.

Wait a minute.

How did my tiny little body react to normal sized germs? Was this something they covered and I just wasn't paying attention? Were my white blood cells really really small now? Were the normal sized germs going to push them around like normal sized people bullied me? Or were they the same size and I just had less blood? Either way I didn't like my chances.

Or the ginormous lump on my back.

"From Sheena to Quasimodo." I said rubbing the tight tender flesh. It felt warm to the touch. That couldn't be a good thing. "I need a machete. And toilet paper. And some Off. And a doctor."

The day was just getting shittier and shittier. My back was throbbing and I was terrified of running into anything that might try to take a bigger bite out of me. But the sun was going down and I was even more scared of being alone in the woods at night. It was not a safe place to play dolly in the dark.

I didn't hesitate taking my bra off at the next trail marker point. It wasn't like it was my last strip poker chip, but I was saving the socks for last. I'm a Netflix and couch kind of gal and walking in the woods barefoot wasn't that appealing to me. And it would just be weird walking around bottomless while I still had my bra on. Besides, my swelling hump was pulling the straps tight causing both my back and boobs to feel super uncomfortable. It wound up in a pile in the hunter's footprint and I let out a sigh of relief as everything came spilling free.

Even without a watch I could tell it was taking me longer and longer to find the next bingo on the trail. Part of it was just me wearing down. It had been forever since I ate or had a real rest. To say nothing of my run-in with the flying blood bank. I was running on adrenaline and I was running out.

I was also running out of light. It was getting harder and harder to find the trail in the growing gloom and I still hadn't found Jordan. How long did it take a trail to grow cold? I couldn't even say for certain that I was following the guy who downed the drone. For all I knew I was hot on the trail of an octogenarian nudist with anxiety disorders.

It was twilight by the time I threw my left sock into the crater of a concealed footprint. That was it, I was naked as the day I was born and about a fifth the size. I was officially out of strip poker chip bread crumbs.

"Now what?"

You're leaving a trail for a blood hound.

"So?"

He's smelling your bread crumbs, not looking at them.

"Oh." I said. That segued into a "Ewwww." when what I was telling myself fully dawned on me.

I could feel my inner voice shrug.

I somehow managed to not get lost finding the next trail marking point. I found the odd indentation under the grass, squatted down, and marked the trail the only way I was able.

"Mom would be so proud of me, peeing in a serial killer's foot print. God, I hope they don't use that as the title of my Lifetime movie. That would be soooo embarrassing."

I used a blade of grass the size of a palm tree to wipe myself. It felt like running high grit sandpaper over my sensitive lady parts and it wasn't absorbent. At all.

I made it to the next footprint. Don't ask me how. There was zero light and I was freaking out cause there still wasn't any sign of Jordan, the hunter, Bertie, or civilization. I'd done the best I could and I had failed epically.

I was stranded in the middle of the scariest giant fairy tale forest never imagined with monsters that would make the Big Bad Wolf pee his pants and run. The sun had fully set and I couldn't even see the moon or stars through the trees. If they were giving off light none of it was making it to my little eyes. I was exposed, scared, exhausted, starving, and shivering.

I couldn't get the moss beneath me to cover me so I had to use grass for a blanket. I wasn't strong enough to rip off bits of grass from the blade. I was having trouble enough just pulling the tall grass down on top of me. Even then it didn't want to stay in place. I finally shoved some blades under me and rolled over onto them. My weight kept them from flying back up.

Barely.

The rough grass rubbed my shivering skin raw. If I survived the malaria I'd need a skin graft when I got out of there. The grass blanket wasn't that warm either. Sure it kept the wind off my exposed little body, but the plant fibers seemed to suck the warmth out of me. But it was the best blanket I was going to get. Better than I deserved. I had royally screwed up my escape plan and now Jordan was somewhere watching some crazy with a hunting license dance around in her freshly flayed skin.

And I was going to die alone in the dark cause I just said no to that Girl Scout membership drive back when I was eight.

"Calm down, Becks. This is gonna be fine. Bertie will be here any minute now. You left a good trail and he can track a falcon on a cloudy day. You're practically saved."

You don't know he's a good tracker.

"He's Mister Great Outdoors. Of course he's a great tracker. Whoever heard of a groundskeeper who gets lost on the grounds?"

This is different. For this he'll need that bloodhound we've been talking about. I don't hear any barks. Do you?

"He'll get one … I mean he's got one. That's what's taken him so long. It's not like there's a Bloodhounds 'r Us on every corner. He had to make some calls. Work the groundskeeper connections."

Maybe.

"I left a trail; he'll find it. End of story."

You did leave a mighty fine trail.

"Bertie won't have any trouble finding me."

Bertie's not the only thing that can follow a trail.

"Shut up!"

I read somewhere that most predators hunt at night.

"I hate you."

The feeling's mutual.

I'm not going to say the night passed uneventfully. I'm just going to say that it passed and I survived. Bertie didn't show up, but neither did some Becky-hungry forest monster. My mini-hunchback wouldn't let me lay on my back, but that didn't matter; I didn't get any sleep that night. The couple of times I half nodded off I ended up waking up convinced that some large, very hungry, tongue was dancing along the soles of my feet.

I looked into the darkness at the spot I last remembered seeing the light. Which was stupid. That was where the sun had set. It was going to rise on the opposite end of my little world. I knew this, but I kept looking at where the sun had gone and thinking about what Tina was doing and what was being done to Jordan.

It got colder. Not so cold I could see my own breath, but I couldn't see anything anyway. I wrapped myself into a ball and tried to squeeze myself warm. I rocked back and forth some, but that only helped a little.

After a very long time I could feel a faint glimmer of light behind me. Warm light. Not much. Not enough. Not yet.

Everything sucked in the coming warmth. The grass around me. The ground beneath. My skin. I could feel dew starting to form on my skin. I'd never had that happen to me before. Was it because I was so small, or would this have happened to me if I were still my normal size? I watched my bare skin in the pre-dawn light. Watched as drops of water the size of golf balls formed on me. My body felt cold and clammy, but my mind was floating a hundred miles above watching this strange thing happen.

I lowered my face to my shoulder and pushed my mouth onto one of those giant water droplets. My teeth broke the water tension and cold liquid slid down my throat. It was the most delicious thing I had ever tasted.

I drank until I couldn't drink any more. The drops that formed on the grass had a greenish tint to them so I only drank the water that formed on me. I cupped the drops in my hands and brought it to my lips. My tummy appreciated having something in it, but it was already rumbling for something more substantial.

In a while it was light enough to really see. I made a point of looking up at the canopy of leaves above me. At the nightmare trees that were freaking me out. I needed to acclimate to them. Maybe if I took them in in small chunks I wouldn't freak out so much.

I left a fresh "trail marker" and moved on to the next footprint.

I almost didn't find it. The morning dew had weighed down the grass enough to nearly cover it up completely. And the mark wasn't as distinct and fresh as it had been yesterday. The trail was definitely going cold.

"What the eff do I do now?"

Follow the trail, numb buts.

"I'm fresh out of breadcrumbs and pee."

So?

"So, I can't make a trail."

Don't.

"How's Bertie going to find us if we don't?"

Either you find Jordan or nobody finds Jordan. Worry about leaving a trail after you know where she is.

I had a point.

I pushed on.

Lucky for me I didn't see and nuts, berries, or any other edible looking plants. I was stupid hungry and would have tried anything no matter how bad an idea it was. With the way my luck had been going any poison I ate wouldn't outright kill me, just make what was left of my life retching agony.

I'd been trail hunting for a good long while before I started looking at a beetle in a way I never thought I would. At least I think it was a beetle. It was the size of my hand, had a brown pill shaped carapace, and was walking around on a bunch of legs I couldn't see.

"You look like a trilobite." I said down to one that was crawling around on the ground I was trail-hunting. "I'm pretty sure my cave-woman ancestors used to eat yours. Evolutionarily speaking your … what … three steps away from being a lobster? And people go nuts for them."

I tamped down the ick-factor and reached down to touch it. As soon as my fingers touched its soft carapace it stopped dead in its tracks.

"Just like a lobster. A super advanced land lobster."

I pinched my fingers around its sides. I almost let go when it began to scream. It was this high pitched wail that hurt my ears, but only lasted a few seconds. I pulled myself together and picked it up.

"You're a lot lighter than I thought you'd be, little guy."

I was handling it. Pretty well if I do say so myself. I just kept telling myself *it's just like a lobster* and I was starting to believe me.

Then I turned it around and got a look under the shell.

It wasn't a beetle. I'm not sure what it was, but whatever it was it had way too many legs to be a beetle. Dozens of legs. Little and writhing. Trying to find something to hold onto. And I swear it's eyes were as big as mine only all black and filled with hate.

I dropped it like an abusive girlfriend and watched it fly away screaming.

"It's not like I had a pot of hot water to cook him in." I tried to console myself.

I found a small sapling and climbed up. I'd been at this all day yesterday and part of today, maybe I was getting close to wherever this trail ended. I needed to get a better look around me and the sapling was easily triple my height. It wasn't an easy climb, but it was easier after going through Bootcamp Lauren.

Just don't tell her I said that. She's enough of a dick.

I didn't see Jordan. Or the hunter. Or Bertie. What I did see made me wonder if there was such a thing as a forest mirage.

It's a trap.

"It's a Milky Way."

Sure enough there was my third favorite candy bar in the entire world just laying there a couple (of my) football fields away.

It's a trap.

"I can see the wrapper. It's still in the wrapper. That means bugs haven't gotten to it yet."

It's still a trap.

"Somebody must have dropped it here. Maybe the hunter. Or … or Bertie. I bet he's been tracking us all night and he bent down to Aragorn the ground and a delicious Milky Way fell out of his jacket pocket."

That doesn't make any sense.

"Or maybe I've left the estate and wandered into some sort of park. There could be a picnic area just around that corner. That means people. With phones. Who can call for help."

Fine. Don't listen to me.

I slid down the sapling like it was a fire pole. Which wasn't such a hot idea without grease. Or pants. But I was too excited to let a little second degree bark burn slow me down. I was hobble running towards the candy as soon as my feet touched ground.

I pushed and strained through the heavy brush until I made it to the clearing it was resting in. The ground felt a bit odd beneath my feet. I couldn't see the dirt from all the cut up, almost mulched, grass.

"Candy and gardening. I must be getting closer to civilization."

The grass cutting alternately cut and tickled my feet so I had to take baby steps the rest of the way to a candy bar that was bigger than me.

"You are so god damn beautiful." I said to the candy. "I could hollow you out and use you as a coffin."

You'll have to get the wrapper off first. Assuming you have time. Cause IT'S A TRAP!

"Shut up, Ackbar."

My inner voice was right about one thing – the wrapper was going to be tricky. At my size it was like trying to rip through a sealed tarp with my bare hands. And it was wet. Sticky wet. Not chocolate sticky. More like sugar water had dried on it. I tried attacking it from every angle I could with my feet on the ground with zero success.

I climbed on top of it trying to find some weakness in its

impenetrable defense. I could feel the chocolate coating shift slightly under the wrapper as it began to melt from my body heat.I could smell the candy underneath and I was drooling to make Pavlov proud.

That's when I felt the first wave of dizziness.

My feet were starting to go numb. I could barely feel the sticky wrapper or the melting chocolate any more.

"This … this isn't good."

I fell backwards onto the cut grass beside my prize. I didn't even feel it when I hit the ground. I just looked up in the air and saw three cage walls lift themselves out of the cut grass and close above me. I was in a pyramid cage and I didn't see a door. And I was pretty sure I'd been drugged by the sticky stuff.

"It really was a trap." I said as everything started to go black.

No shit, Sherlock.

Nine: Music Box Dancer

I woke up in stages.

The first thing I was aware of was trying to count how many times I'd been drugged unconscious, but I kept losing count and starting over. My sleepy brain was getting confused about when my many drug-outs occurred. I had a vivid memory of Maria slipping some shrinking/knock out drugs into my prom punch. Or the time I was a babysitter for Lauren and I got blind drunk and shrunk.

"Owwww."

I'd woken up enough to feel a hot throbbing pain on both of my butt cheeks. Like someone had spanked me with a hot steam iron.

"That's not where the vampire bit me." I was still groggy, but waking up.

I was laying on my front with my arms folded under me and my face pressed to the wooden floor. My mouth was half open and it tasted like something had crawled inside, found a life partner, had babies, and became the forebears of a long line that eventually abandoned their wet cave when it got too gross.

I flailed a hand out from under me and groped around the area my butt should be. My half awake hand landed on my upper legs, lower back, and hips before finally finding my smarting tush. I could feel sore raised skin under the tights and underwear I was wearing.

What?

"Wait … no. I left a trail." My voice was slow and sleepy, but more awake than I was. "And I wasn't wearing tights."

My hand flapped its way up my back. Well, it tried. There was something stiff but soft rising up from my lower back. I pushed it down, but as soon as I let my hand go it sprang up again.

I had a tail!

No. It went all the way around my waist. Like someone had built a lace wall around my middle. This was too much for me to process right now so I just flopped my arm over the wall and explored my back.

I could feel the mosquito hickey under whatever it was I was wearing. It wasn't as big as it had been and it didn't hurt anymore. The skin felt cool through the tight thin fabric. I wasn't sure, but I thought I was in a one piece swimsuit. Or maybe a leotard. But that made the kind of sense that wasn't. I'd started out in full cowgirl cosplay and was buck naked by the time I'd found that Milky Way.

"What the eff?"

I forced my eyes open and my mouth shut. Light poured in from above making the small pool of drool in front of me glisten. It took me a minute for my eyes to focus. Like I said light was coming down on me. Like a spotlight. If there was a spotlight with a billion watt bulb out there. I was in my own little island of light. Maybe twenty feet across. Twenty of my feet, but don't hold me to that math. I'd been through a lot and my brain was still woozy.

Outside my island of bright it was all dark.

"Hello." I called out to the dark. I didn't even get an echo for a reply.

I pushed myself into a sitting position with my other arm. I flipped my legs over so I was laying on my side instead of sitting on my butt. The more I woke up the more it hurt. Sitting down normal wasn't going to be fun. At least the pain was helping me wake up.

I got a good look at me and the ballerina outfit I'd been dressed in. Tutu included.

"Calm down, Becky." I needed to not freak out. "You were alone in the woods and going to die. Some nice person found you and brought you to their home. They treated your vampire assault and did something mysterious to your butt. They saw you were naked so they got you dressed. In a fetish outfit they just happened to have lying around."

I shut up when the music started.

It sounded classical, but cheap. Like something a real ballet dancer might dance to only performed by tin instruments.

Like a music box.

" … uh … thanks for the rescue." I said to the person behind the music. "It must have been weird finding a tiny little naked lady in that trap of yours. Bet you thought you caught a fairy or something, huh. Thanks for using cruelty free by the way.

"I totally get you want me to go all Tiny Dancer, but I'm feeling creeped out right now and I've got a metric butt ton of questions. About why my butt hurts. What happened to my friend, Jordan. A bunch of other stuff. So if you could turn off the music and turn on the lights maybe we could have a chat. Like civilized people."

I heard something flip shut in the darkness and the music stopped. I felt relief wash over me; I'd finally met a normal sized person who was willing to listen to me.

I looked expectantly into the dark waiting for my host to make the next move. I thought I smelled smoke. Then I saw a single point of light grow a brighter and brighter red. Fire, but not an open flame. Then the light started flying at me. I realized in the split second that it was in the air that it was part of a bigger … thing with only one end lit. Like a torch being thrown at me.

I didn't know it was a lit cigarette until it landed in my island of light. It came down hard on the wet end throwing embers and ash all over the place still headed straight towards the spot I was laying in.

SHIT!

I scrambled to my feet, but only managed to get half up by the time it came down on me. It was longer than my arm and thicker than my leg and I was lucky the wet end was what hit my thigh. Another spray of embers erupted from the pile of burning ash that was bigger than my fist. Only this time I was right under it. Dots of fire landed in my hair, on my skin, and on the ballet outfit I'd been dressed in.

By the time I'd stopped, dropped, and rolled the fire out the cigarette torch had bounced off into the dark.

I heard a sizzling crack above me and saw a match flame-on in the darkness and move around. I never smoked, but I'd seen enough old movies to tell my captor had lit another cigarette. I caught a lightning flash glimpse of a face in the cupped match light, but he was shaking the match out before I could make out any details.

I heard the lid pull open and the classy cheap music started again.

I pulled myself to my feet and brought myself into my best impression of a ballet position. The slipper like shoes I was wearing helped me get on my toes and the tutu made me hyper aware of my hips, but I'd never danced ballet. I wasn't built for ballet.

I felt stupid and humiliated twirling around pretending to do something I'd never done. The more I danced the more I realized this wasn't a real ballerina costume. It wasn't even meant to be a doll sized version of a real dance outfit. The neckline was too low. And so tight I was spilling up and out of it. The leotard might not have been a thong, but they weren't doing much to cover my nutcracker.

This was a sexy ballerina outfit. About as subtle as that French maid's costume Amber liked me in.

Only made for a doll. I felt dirty and objectified and fetishy. Not in the fun roleplaying way with Amber. This was different. Wearing this I was meat. Tits and ass and jiggle.

My face was burning by the time the music box wound down and I took my cue to stop dancing. I felt like I was going to explode. I felt hurt and used and pissed, but there wasn't anything I could do but live with it or die burning. I wanted Tina.

No.

I wanted Carly.

"I've danced for you like you wanted. Can't you just tell me if Jordan is all right. I think she's hurt and I'm worried about her. She was being chased by a drone. That's a long story. I found it shot out of the sky by an arrow. I think whoever did it has her. There was blood."

I saw the faint cigarette light bob in the dark getting closer to me. Fast, but not thrown torch fast. I was trying to figure out what was going on when something ginormous was stabbed into the wood table I was standing on. The sudden force knocked me on my ass, spreading my legs apart, and pushing my tutu up ridiculously. I must have looked like Tinkerbelle if Tink got dressed up real slutty and got falling down drunk.

Disney, please don't sue me.

I looked up at the new monolith that now towered over me. Or maybe it was too narrow to be a monolith. I'm not really an expert. Whether it counted as a monolith or not was beside the point. It was definitely an arrow. The same type that had taken out the drone.

I was processing that when a giant hand reached into the light and pulled the arrow up and away. The hole it left in the wood was bigger than my spread fingers. Not that I had time to go check that out before the arrow came back. This time stabbed all the way into the table. Right between my legs.

I was already on my ass; there was no place to go but up. I was tossed up into the air and landed flat on my back with my thighs on either side of the shaft.

The music started again.

"Seriously?"

I looked around the giant shaft buried between my legs … Yeah. I know how that sounds. I could see the cigarette fire brighten as my captor inhaled deeply. It gave off exactly enough light for me to see the fingers holding it, but nothing else. The fingers and the fire moved into flicking position.

I got on my toes and started to perform again.

The song was halfway through when I heard the first muffled moans coming from the cigarette mouth. A couple measures later and I heard the unmistakable sound of a zipper going down.

I thought I was going to be sick. It was one thing to know that someone was perving on you. Knowing they were whacking it to you. In the same room. While you couldn't see them. Was way creepier.

I felt like I'd been dipped in a sewer. I tried to ignore it. Just let my mind go to my happy place while my body went through the motions. But every time I was close to getting there I'd hear another stifled moan and I was dipped right back under.

"Work the arrow." The giant's voice was a lot higher than I'd imagined. Like a teenage boy. Or a chain smoking woman. "Use it like a stripper pole."

I didn't have any choice.

I had never stripped either. Not the kind that requires a pole anyway. I faked my way through twirling around the giant arrow. Spinning myself and climbing up it like I'd seen women do in the movies. I hoped that they were getting off to the costume cause I wasn't going to take that off. There are some lines your head won't let you cross. That was one of mine.

It was surreal. Fake stripping to music I'd fake ballet danced to. But my unseen captor didn't seem to mind. He just turned the music back on whenever the song would end. The tinkling of the cheap music drowned out some of the masturbation sounds.

Some.

By the fifth time through the song the breathing became heavier and faster. The groans more urgent. I knew what was coming. I knew who was coming.

If I had anything in my stomach I'd have tossed it.

Then the breathing stopped. I just kept dancing. Forcing myself to go numb. I think I'd have gone crazy if I let myself think about what was happening and all the stupid things I'd done to get here.

This time the music didn't start up again after it stopped. I just stood there holding onto the arrow with one hand not sure what to do next. I crossed the other arm over my chest and pressed my fist under my armpit. I didn't want this perv staring at my stuff while he was coming down from his jerk.

Somewhere along the line he'd lost the cig. So I had no idea where he was. I heard the scrape of a giant chair being pulled out followed by my giant captor shambling around in the dark.

Then the light came on.

The first thing I noticed was that my captor was a she. Definitively. She hadn't bothered pulling her pants up and I had an unobstructed view of her furry vajayjay.

She languidly slid her underwear and jeans up her hips in one fluid motion. She buttoned and zipped as she stared down at me cowering beneath her. I was scared, but I stared back. Not to face my fears. Not to rebel. I wanted to know every line of her face so that I could describe her perfectly for the police sketch artist I was going to find when I got out of here.

She was older than me. Mid-thirties maybe, but she had one of those faces that was hard to say. I could have been five years off either way. She was white, but tanned. Her long dark hair was pulled back into a simple braid that hung over her shoulder. I wanted to Rapunzel my way up it and knock the shit eating grin off her giant bitch mouth.

"Where's my friend?" I finally asked.

"You don't have any." She said in the same throaty voice I'd heard before.

She reached down and picked me up with the same hand she'd been jilling off with. I could feel the warm wetness seeping through the thin material of my dance tights. The heavy scent was earthy and unmistakable and now it was all over me. I found myself reacting to it despite myself. Feeling fear segue into arousal.

What the eff was wrong with me?

"What did you do to me?" I needed to not be thinking those kind of thoughts about this woman. Just because she wasn't the knuckle-dragging subhuman man I thought she was didn't mean she was all sunshine and rainbows either.

She held me up towards her half an arm length from her face. I could almost smell her rotten cigarette breath over the sex scent. I couldn't see her other hand, but I could tell it was reaching for something on her belt. Something she flipped open with a flick of the wrist before bringing it into my line of sight.

"It" was a buck knife.

The blade was bigger than I was. I could see my reflection cowering in the cold flat steel in all my slutty ballerina glory.

I stopped breathing.

"You want to know what I did to your butt?" She asked.

I watched as my reflection nodded up at her.

"Let me show you."

She shifted me around in her hand and brought the giant knife to my foot. The blade was sharp. The tip was filed smaller than my pinky toe and my pinky toe was pretty damn small. I could feel the tip break the surface of the ballet shoe. It didn't touch the tights beneath. I'd have been impressed by her precision if I wasn't scared shitless. The knife made two more butterfly flicks and what was left of the soft shoe fell away.

Three more flicks and I was barefoot except for the tights.

I didn't feel the blade cut into the tights; I just felt the open air on my foot after it was exposed. I spread my toes apart and wriggled them. It felt good. I hated tights. When I pulled my toes back together there was something hard and cold between my littlest toes. I could feel the cool steel of the slat side of the blade. I was a millimeter away from being crippled.

The steel passed between my toes and went up my leg cutting away the cheap nylon tights only barely touching my skin. Not cutting. Just enough to be felt. Like a single metal fingernail running from my ankle to leotard brushing aside the cobweb tights.

The blade followed the edge of the leotard. My captor adjusted me in her hand for easy access until she'd made it all the way around and that leg of the tights fell off. It lay on her palm until she lowered her face over me and blew it off. I choked a little on her rancid breath. The bit of nylon flew away and floated to the floor.

She was peeling me.

I only hoped she'd stop at my clothing.

She repeated the cut on the other leg. The only thing left of the tights was whatever was under the leotard. That wasn't much.

She turned me around so I was looking straight up at her. She held the knife up high pointed down straight at my heart. High for me anyway. It was only a few inches for her. I watched as the blade lowered straight down. So big it was like an Aztec god had stepped down from her pyramid to sacrifice me to her god.

I felt the cool steel on the skin above my heart. I could feel the metal fingernail work its way agonizingly slowly down my body. I felt the cold flat steel on either side of my breasts. I pulled my arms away from my body trying to keep my boobs from pressing up too tightly, but the leotard was designed to give me cleavage.

I felt the pressure on my breasts go away. For a split second I thought they'd been cut off, but the rational part of me (and there is a rational part of me) put two and two together. The cleavage creating leotard had been cut, not me. The tip made a straight slow line to my navel and paused there. I swear I could feel the tiny tip slip inside and rest there.

All this time I'd been staring up at her big dumb face. Watching the look in her eyes as she revealed more and more of me. Watching her get off to my reactions. I turned my head down and looked at my torso. Stared at the line the knife had passed through. I expected to see my chest cut wide open. I thought I'd see parts of me I never wanted to see. In glorious technicolor. But all I saw was a half cut away leotard and an almost invisible scratch line.

She continued downward.

She didn't bother cutting around the nothing that remained of the tights. When she got to that point she just cut through both layers at once. I could feel the tip work its way closer and closer to my lady parts. I closed my eyes and tried to blot out what was happening. It was the most intimately horrible twenty seconds of my life.

She didn't bother taking the knife away. No. It was easier for her to just flip me over in her hand when she needed to. And she kept the blade as close to my skin as she could just to add to my humiliation.

I was kneeling on the palm of her hand when she reached the end of her long cut. The leotard fell in two pieces on either side of me. The only part that was even close to still being on me was the bunched down sleeves and I pulled those off fast before she could try to cut them away as well.

She dropped me on the table and walked across the room for something. By the time I pulled myself to my feet she'd come back with a hand mirror bigger than my entire body. She put it on the table and took a seat.

"You want to know why you're butthurt, take a look." She said, putting her booted feet on the table.

I turned my hurting butt towards the mirror as she watched. She was looking for a reaction. She got one.

"YOU BRANDED ME!"

"I mark all my property."

"I'm a human being, for Christ's sake. Not cattle."

"Not with udders like that."

"Cause big boobs equal fat cow. I get it."

She gave out one long throaty 'MOOOOOOOO" as she picked me up and carried me away.

She opened a door and we were outside. I stared up into the same impossible sky I'd seen outside Maria's mansion, poking a hole through the canopy of the nightmare trees. It might have been the same woods. Or the giant psycho might have taken me three states away. The sun was out, but I didn't think it was the same day. She could have taken me anywhere while I was drugged.

We'd just left some sort of out building hidden beside a copse of trees. I think it was a little bigger than a shed, but my sense of scale wasn't that strong. I'd spent most of my life pretty much as tall as I used to be. I'd only been tiny for a few weeks; as far as I was concerned we'd just come out of something the size of a gutted out office building.

She placed me down on a stump. She took a seat on the ground beside it putting her giant face level with my small body.

"Take a seat, Rebecca." She ordered. Her tone was neutral at least.

"How do you know my name? Did you give me truth serum while I was out? Cause that stuff doesn't work and I'm pretty sure it's illegal. And none of it is admissible. Anywhere."

"Jordan told me, moron."

"Oh."

"We need to have a little talk."

"Is Jordan all right?" I asked. Part of me was worried for her; part of me was worried about what would happen to me if she wasn't ok.

"Let me tell you a little 'once upon a time,' little girl."

She moved her face even closer to me until her lips almost brushed my tummy and boobs when she spoke. I didn't even come up to her nose. I could feel hot angry air blow down on me from the nostrils above my head. I looked up into them and freaked out a little. Again. My life had become one big meltdown ever since I shrank. This whole upnostril thing was just the tip of the iceberg.

I took a step back and tripped on the uneven stump wood. My feet went out from under me and I came crashing down on my already sore butt. I screamed a little as my full weight came down on the rough wood. My ass felt like it had landed on an electric fence. I started to pull myself up, but was stopped by a powerful "No" from my giant captor. Her cigarette breath washed over me and I felt sick.

But I stayed sitting.

"Once upon a time there was a hunter who lived in the middle of nowhere." She said as I fumed. Even stepped back I was barely able to see her eyes from where I was. "Every day she would go out hunting and trapping to keep herself alive.

"Then one day the hunter tracked a twelve point buck for more than two miles. She crossed onto somebody else's property, but that didn't matter to the hunter. The buck didn't belong to the person who owned the land; he belonged to himself. Or the woman who could bring him down.

"She saw him standing there resting beside a gnarled old spruce and she prepared to take her shot. She used a longbow cause that's the way her father had taught her to hunt and she still thought the old ways worked best. She knocked an arrow into her bow, lined up her shot, and got ready to fire.

"But something happened and the arrow wasn't fired. Not at the deer. The buck heard it before the hunter did. A whirring noise that spooked the animal. The hunter probably could have made the kill, but it wouldn't have been clean. So she let him bolt and waited to see what had scared him off.

"And then a beautiful princess ran into view. The most beautiful princess the hunter had ever seen. Only someone had taken away her beautiful dresses and forced her to run naked through the dark scary woods.

"Do you like my fairy tale so far?"

"Not so much the Brothers Grimm as 'Dear Penthouse Forum.'" I hadn't realized I'd said that out loud until I spoke the last word. "Also really really creepy."

"The princess was being followed by a metal monster that flew without wings. She was running terrified through the strange woods looking for someone to save her from the weird beast. That's when the hunter fired her arrow."

She stopped talking then. Leaving it open as to whether she shot the princess or the monster. I found an arrow punched through the drone so I knew the answer to that question, but I really doubted psycho hunter ever went hunting with only one arrow. Had she shot Jordan too? There was a lot of blood. But Jordan had to be alive if she told this bitch my name.

Unless she bled out later.

"What happened then? Is Jordan OK? You didn't shoot her did you?" The words came rushing out of me even faster than normal.

"Of course I didn't shoot her." The giant sounded offended at the thought.

"There was blood where she fell. Lots of it."

"There was some blood. Some. Not lots. As small as you are you can't tell the difference between a puddle and a pond. Jordan never went outside barefoot a day in her life. Then some asshole made her run naked through strange woods."

"Oh." I felt like shit.

"Her feet were raw by the time she collapsed in front of me. I had to carry her back to my cabin kicking and screaming that she couldn't leave her precious 'Goddess Rebecca' behind."

"Do you even know what consent is?" I asked.

"I know you almost got her killed."

"Yeah … well …" I didn't have an answer.

"I figured she'd escaped from an asylum when she told me you were only a few inches tall. Then I took her collar off and found a saddle attached to the back. She told me what she knows while I got her fixed up."

"I can explain everything."

"Don't bother; I don't care. If it were up to me you'd still be out there dead or on your way to being dead. It's what you deserve for almost getting her killed."

"That's not fair. I was …"

"But Jordan cried and begged me to go out and find you. She was so worried about what would happen to you in the great dark woods. She made me promise to find you. I got lucky and you found one of the traps I'd left for you. I don't think I could stand to see the look on her face if I told her you were dead."

"That was for me? Specifically for me?"

"I'd never bait an animal trap with a candy bar. I'm just lucky you have shit impulse control."

"Wait." It had taken my brain a bit to read between the lines of what she'd been saying. "Are you in love with Jordan?"

"Yes."

"Cause that wasn't crazy fast or anything."

"The heart wants what it wants." She said.

"Whose heart wanted to peel me out of some slutty ballerina cosplay? After fapping off?"

"That's part of your punishment."

"I don't know what word bothers me more in that sentence, punishment or part." I said. "And look. Things almost ended up really really bad, but if it wasn't for me you'd have never met Jordan. So that's good, isn't it?"

"This is how it's going to be, Becky. Jordan is awake, but a long way from being fully recovered. I'm going to take you in to see her. She'll like that. You won't tell her what I did to you in the shed."

"Why not?" I didn't think I was going to like the answer to this.

"Because it will upset her. And your next punishment will be fatal."

"You are totes bluffing." I said. "If she's that wound up and you love her as much as you say you do there's no way you'd do that."

"Try me."

She just stared down at me with a perfect poker face the size of a house.

"I won't tell her." I finally said.

"Or about any of the other punishment sessions we'll have in the shed."

"ok"

"Good."

She slowly straightened herself up. I just sat there on my throbbing butt as I watched more and more of her rise up into the air. Like the star destroyer opening in Star Wars if the star destroyer was a woman in jeans and a t-shirt. I wasn't able to see her face when she finally stopped. She wiped her masturbation coated hand on her pants then picked me up again.

Jordan was in bed when my unnamed captor carried me over the threshold of her cabin. The place looked primitive, but neat. Everything was in one huge central room. Living room. Kitchen. Bedroom. If there was a bathroom I didn't see it. Organized in the way years that watching serial killer movies had prepared me for.

"Stella, you found her." Jordan's voice sounded weak, but happy. As effed up as this situation was she was at least one of us had retained her innocence.

Also the woman who'd just rubbed one out watching me dance was named Stella.

"She found one of my cruelty free traps." Stella said. "She was suffering from mild exposure and a nasty bug bite, but I've taken good care of her while you've been here healing. Haven't I, Becky?"

"A ha." I just nodded my head and tried not to think about it.

"I'm so glad." Jordan said. "Can you spend some time with me,

Goddess? I know I shouldn't be asking, but I've missed you so much. I was so scared that you'd be carried off by an owl or drown in a pond."

"Actually there's something Becky wants to do for you. Isn't there, Becky?"

I just stared at her dumbly. We hadn't talked about this.

"Becky feels responsible for you getting yourself hurt." Stella said before I had a chance to contradict her. "She wants to make it up to you by kissing every cut on your poor little feet. She won't take no for an answer and she refuses to eat until she's done."

"Goddess?"

Jordan looked at me like she wasn't sure what to do. Not like I had any better idea what to do. Maybe it was the drug on the Milky Way, maybe it was the fear of waking up in the clutches of a madwoman, but I'd barely noticed my hunger until Stella mentioned food. Then my stomach reminded me how loud it could growl when I didn't feed it.

Stella looked at me with a "don't fuck this up for me" expression.

"Yes." I finally said. "I'm very sorry to have gotten you hurt and scared. Please let me make it up to you by doing this."

I sounded as convincing as a little girl who got caught doing something naughty who then was forced to apologize by her mom. There was no way Jordan was going to buy this.

"Of course." Jordan said.

Crap.

Stella pulled Jordan's feet out from under the covers. They were covered in white gauze and bandages. Stella popped me down on the bed in front of Jordan's feet and started the lengthy unwrap period.

I watched the slow reveal with dread. I wasn't looking forward to doing this, but it looked like Stella was hell bent on punishing me for what I'd done to her Stockholm Syndrome girlfriend. Maybe I could get this over with fast and get something to quiet my tummy.

Then I got a look at the skin under the gauze and I didn't want to eat anything again ever.

They were red and bloody. No. Not bloody. Just moist in the pre-scabby way things get when you take the bandages off too soon. I watched as more and more of Jordan's poor feet were exposed to the air. I could see them glisten grossly in the light. I saw the red-brown stains on the white gauze.

I'd done that to her.

I felt like shit. And I kept on feeling shittier and shittier with every centimeter that was exposed. Why did I have to try to run away like that? With no plan just the hope that things would work out even though I hadn't thought anything through? That was pretty much the story of my life. Letting myself do what seemed like a good idea at the time only to have it go pear shaped once all the pieces fell into place. It had ruined my relationships. It had gotten me shrunk. And now it had scarred a woman who'd wanted to be hurt, but not like that.

Maybe I deserved what Stella was doing to me.

I should have listened to Carly. Jail would have sucked, but I'd have gotten out eventually and Jordan never would have gotten hurt. I had been so stupid and thoughtless and now I was going to have to pay the price.

Jordan's upright foot towered over me. There was a hierarchy of cuts. The soles of her feet were almost entirely cut raw, but there were deeper cuts that left distinct marks over the rest.

"Will she be able to walk again?" I asked Stella. I didn't look up, I couldn't look her in the eyes.

"In a while." Stella said. "I cleaned the wounds and put some Silvadene on em. And gave her an oral antibiotic. There's no sign of infection. The skin will heal, but it will take time. It'll hurt to put any weight on them for a bit. There will be scars."

I just looked at what I'd done. I started crying, but I didn't know for sure if either of the giant women could see my tiny tears.

"I'm afraid I can't let you kiss her wounds after all, Becky." Stella said. "I'm not sure that would be safe for Jordan or you. I know you wanted to make it up to her, but not while everything is so fresh. I'll just put on a fresh coat of Silvadene and wrap them back up."

Stella knew she wasn't going to make me kiss Jordan's feet before she undid the bandages. She just wanted me to see the consequences of my bad decisions. Rub my stupidity in my face. Punish me by putting me up to a mirror and showing how ugly I was. And she was right.

"can I do it" I said the words so soft I didn't hear them.

"What?"

"Can I rub the cream on her feet?" I asked, louder this time.

"At your size that'd be like painting a house." Stella said. "It'll be hard work and you won't be finished till after sundown."

"I understand." I said. I did my best to ignore my aching hunger.

"Alright then."

"You don't have to, Goddess." Jordan finally added her two cents. "I can do it myself while Stella gets you something to eat. You must be very hungry."

"It's alright. I can eat later." I said. "I'm very sorry that I ended up getting you hurt. I didn't want this to happen, but sometimes things kinda … don't work out for me. I'm sorry you had to get caught in the crossfire of my bad decision. I'm going to do this for you so just lay back and let me get to work. That's an order."

"Yes, my Goddess."

Jordan lay back down. Stella put the open jar of cream at the foot of the bed where I could access it.

I got to work.

Stella was right. It wasn't easy. I'm not even sure if it was safe for me to be touching as much of the stuff as I was, but my need to expiate my guilt outweighed any worries about my own health.

I dipped my hands into the thick, cold, cream and pulled up as much of it as I could. It looked like a lot in my tiny hands, but didn't cover much of Jordan's hurting soles. It was going to take dozens of trips, maybe a couple hundred, to bring over enough to the white goop to cover all the damaged skin.

Jordan was asleep and the sun had set by the time I'd finished. It had taken me so long the first foot and half of the second had already dried. Stella showed me (and Jordan) some mercy by applying another coat herself. It took her less than a minute to do what had taken me hours to accomplish. Another five minutes to put on fresh dressings.

I was exhausted and starving, but I felt better.

Stella picked me up and deposited me in a bird cage hanging in the center of the room. There was a bottle cap of water and a slice of bread. Stella turned out the light and climbed into bed with Jordan. I ate until I fell asleep on my giant bread mattress.

Ten: Cabin In The Woods

I was worried that Stella was going to take me for regular punishment/get off sessions in the wood shed, but that didn't happen. Maybe she knew how shitty I felt after seeing Jordan's poor feet. Maybe she thought I'd learned my lesson after I'd exhausted myself trying to make Jordan's pain go away. Maybe she was waiting for her next shipment from kinkydollywear.com. Mostly I think she was too focused on Jordan to pay that much attention to me.

I was left in my bird cage without any orders to follow or any real idea what to do. I was given food and fresh water. That kept me busy for maybe half an hour each day. If I lingered over it. I had a makeshift toilet that was probably closer to a real bathroom than what the normal women had to work with. Not like that was something to take up scads and scads of my time.

There was no cable or internet. If Stella had a radio she never turned it on. The cage had exactly one thing to do for entertainment, but I didn't have the wings to fly up to the swinging perch. Besides, it reminded me of my first session with Jordan and the thought of that weirded me out. Even bashing myself for all the horrible mistakes I'd made got old fast.

With nothing better to do I watched Stella court Jordan.

It's hard to describe out relationship. To Jordan I was still her "Goddess," but it was obvious that Stella owned me. Stella was an alpha female while I barely registered as a beta pet girl. Jordan may have taken orders from me, but she knew I took orders from Stella. After awhile she stopped looking to me to relay Stella's orders and just got it straight from the domme's mouth. I had no idea how that was playing into Jordan's fantasy, but she seemed happy. After what I'd put her through I wasn't about to rock that boat.

There was something about the way Stella treated Jordan that I found … I don't want to say sweet cause there's still that weird vibe about how we came here.

Stella sorta saved us. But if she hadn't been there the drone would have led Bertie to Jordan and she would have been fine. Maybe I'd have been found. I'm not sure how pissed off vindictive Maria could get, but I don't think she would have left me out there to die no matter how bad I'd fucked up.

The way things worked out Stella had some plausible deniability going. A reasonable person could say that she rescued us in the woods. Fine. But she hadn't made any effort to get Jordan or me back to civilization. Or even let anyone know that we were all right. Stella was taking care of Jordan's injuries, but there's no way Jordan wouldn't have done better off in a hospital.

Every day we were there it became harder and harder to give Stella any benefit of the doubt. It was pretty obvious that we were prisoners. My cage was obvious. Jordan's was her injury. As she started to heal Stella was making a subtler prison. And it was working. Jordan never asked to go back. I don't know how Stella would have responded to that if she had.

I'm pretty sure I knew how it would go if I asked. If I was lucky Stella'd just say no. If she was feeling mean she'd just take me out to the middle of the woods and let me die on my own. So I never asked either.

If you could ignore all that. If you could put aside how Jordan and I got here and all the fucked up shit that happened in the woodshed. And my being branded. If you could do that bit of mental gymnastics. You'd say that Stella treated Jordan sweetly.

Take that with a pillar of salt.

Stella did everything for Jordan. Cooked. Fed her. Carried her to the outhouse. Kept her company while she was awake. Watched over her when she slept. She didn't do everything Jordan asked, but she did enough.

And each night Stella would turn off the lamp and climb into bed with her. The first couple of nights they just talked themselves to sleep. The third night I could hear them doing more than talking. My imagination filled in the parts I could only hear. And I could hear everything.

I'm not going to defend myself too hard, but it was impossible to be in that room and not think sexy thoughts. Not with what I was hearing/imagining. My hand took the scenic route from my neck to my lady parts and I rubbed one out while the giant love birds consummated their love somewhere in the dark below me.

They were still going at it when I was finished. I felt guilty for spying on them. Even if I had no way of ignoring them and was so bored I needed something, anything, to keep me from going batshit insane.

Then I realized I didn't matter to them. Not like a real person. I was a pet. You didn't worry if your goldfish could hear you going down on each other. You weren't worried if your cat knew you were getting busy. I was beneath them even while I was suspended above their heads.

That was a hard thing to face. Being able to be ignored. To have my existence compartmentalized to such a point that it didn't matter if I was there or not. To be less than an afterthought.

Then I remembered Stella jilling off while I danced to the song from her music box.

I didn't masturbate again. Not for the rest of the time I was in Stella's cabin.

I'd been there five days.

Five days of waking up in my cage, eating, using my thimble toilet, and watching the woman who owned me seduce the woman who bought me. Life as Stella's pet sucked.

Day six was going to be different. I could tell the moment I woke up and dragged myself to the thimble. Stella was awake. It seemed like she was always awake. I fell asleep listening to her sweet talk Jordan and woke up to see her strut around the cabin like she owned the place. Which I suppose she did, but that was beside the point.

Stella was awake and getting dressed as normal, but so was Jordan. I don't think Jordan had worn anything other than a sheet and a smile since we'd gotten here. But there she was rolling up the cuffs of a pair of Stella's too large jeans and sliding a t-shirt long enough to be a dress over her head. Her bandages more or less filled out the oversized socks she was wearing. If you didn't know any better you might have thought she was the shrunken woman.

Jordan stood up. More or less. I was pretty sure more of her weight was resting on the table she was next to than her feet, but she was upright. And that had to be a good thing. I saw her wince when she took a step, but she only did that when Stella wasn't looking. When she was Jordan put on a brave face.

They'd been talking lowly between them. Jordan looked scared and nervous. Stella just looked like she always did – three seconds away from either a cracking a shit eating grin or hitting you with the back of her meaty fist.

Whatever they were talking about ended when Jordan looked over in my direction. Even I could read the guilt on her body language. Stella saw it and stopped talking.

The hunter crossed the few feet to my cage, opened the door, and just Fay Wrayed me out. I didn't bother struggling. There was no point in delaying the inevitable. Whatever the inevitable might be. Besides, her warm fingers actually felt nice against my bare skin. I hadn't noticed how cold it was in there until I felt her heat wrap around me.

I was giant carried over to Jordan. Her look of guilt intensified as I got closer.

"You're not thinking about putting me down, are you?" I'd meant it as a joke, but no one laughed. "Like Ol' Yeller. Not like on the table."

"We're about to tell you how things are going to be from now on, Becky." Stella said in a tone that wasn't exactly thrilling me. "Why don't you start, honey."

The last part was directed at Jordan who looked like a stage fright victim who forgot to read the script.

"... umm … ah … It's just that Stella … Stella can't stay here all the time, Becky. She … ah … needs to go hunting and … um … get supplies. And you see she doesn't think it's a good idea for me to take orders from you after what happened in the woods. And I don't either."

"What Jordan is trying to say is there's going to be a new chain of command." Stella broke the awkward silence. "And you're not going to be at the top anymore."

I could feel my stomach sink when Jordan called me Becky instead of Goddess. Stella's words just drove a nail into the coffin. OK. That's a horrible mixed metaphor, but I was reeling from this. I know it's going to sound stupid, but it got to me. Deep. I know I'd just spent the last few days being an ignored pet, but there was still some uncertainty about where I stood with Jordan. My power over her was the only power I had left. Part of me knew that it was all fake, that the only power I had was what Jordan let me have, but it still felt shitty to lose it.

"okay"

I said the word in a very small voice. I knew it didn't matter if I agreed or not; the decision was made.

"We'll start with the basics." Stella went on. "I am in charge. When I am away Jordan is in charge. If we both have to be away at the same time you'll be locked in your cage where you can't get into any trouble. Is that clear?"

"Yes, ma'am."

"I'm going to be gone for some time. I don't expect you to be any trouble for your new mistress." Stella handed me to Jordan and bent down to give her a kiss. "I'll be back soon. If she tries to give you any trouble let me know. I'll take her to the wood shed later."

Jordan shook her head submissively. Stella grabbed her long bow and arrows and left.

Jordan's hand was shaking so badly my teeth were chattering.

"I know I'm not supposed to give the orders any more, but maybe it would be better if you put me down."

"Yeah. Good idea."

I wasn't so much deposited on the table as dropped there. Then Jordan collapsed herself into a chair. Her sigh of relief almost blew me over.

OK. I'm exaggerating. I'm not **that** small.

"Are you ok?" I asked.

"No." She said after catching her breath. "But it's getting better."

"I'm so sorry I did that to you. If I'd have know it was going to work out like that I'd have never tried anything so stupid."

" … it's … it's ok. We can't change what was, we can only manage the consequences. Besides I'd have never met Stella if we hadn't made a run for it like that." Jordan smiled through her pain like a true submissive.

"Look. This is probably none of my business buuutttttttt it's a small cabin and there's only the one room. You don't have to be some peeping Tom perv to figure out that you and the great white hunter have been rubbing uglies. And there's nothing wrong with that. She's pretty. And confident. And the whole setup has to be pushing your sub buttons. But what I'd like to know is, do you love her?"

Jordan stared down at a random spot on the table while she thought about that. I walked over to the butter dish and took a seat.

"Maybe." She said after a very long time.

"Okay."

"I like what she does for me."

"I can tell."

"Not just in bed. The whole package. How many people get rescued in the woods by hunter and carried off to her cabin? It's like something out of a fairy tale."

"I heard that somewhere else."

"She treats me so well. She's so tender and gentle with me. Her hands … her hands are just so soft and nimble. When she changes my bandages I never feel her touch me. Just the bandages. I can close my eyes and pretend that she's a ghost come back to look over me."

"A guardian angel with benefits?" I asked.

"Yeah. I guess."

"She sounds perfect."

Jordan just sat there quietly. I wanted to tell her about what happened in the shed. Wanted to tell her that Stella got that gentle touch skinning animals and she came close to skinning me. Wanted to let her know that her perfect woman got off torturing and humiliating me. But I was scared she'd tell Stella and that would be the end of me.

"I think there's something wrong with Stella." Jordan said after her long pause. "I think she's broken inside."

"That's … uh …" Did I tell her what I knew? I wanted to, but my decision making track record hadn't been that great lately.

"Have you ever looked her straight in the eyes?" Jordan asked. I nodded. "There's something … I don't like what I see there."

"Then why?"

"Do I let her fuck me?"

"Among other things."

"Cause when the lights are out I can't see her eyes. I'm scared and alone and no one knows I'm here except you. And you don't count. She touches me and her ghost hands feel so good I just bury any doubts and let her … you know."

"Yeah. Look … Jordan there's something I …"

There was a knock on the cabin door.

We were in a cabin in the middle of I had no idea where. No one knew we were here except for Stella.

There was another knock.

"What do we do?" Jordan asked, clearly not getting the spirit of Stella's "you're in charge while I'm gone" speech.

"Who died and made me the grown up?"

Jordan looked like she wanted to do a thousand things at once and most of them involved hiding. The third knock made her decision. She reached out and picked me up with her right hand while lifting the lid off the sugar bowl with her left. I was lifted a few inches into the air, moved about a foot to the left, and dropped into the sugar bowl.

"HEY!"

My cry was muffled by the lid being dropped back on the bowl and Jordan stumbling to her feet. I tried to push the lid up, but it was a lot heavier than me. I pushed and pushed but all that happened was my feet started sinking in the fine white sugar. I stopped pushing just before my knees got covered, but even that didn't stop me from sinking.

I was up to my thigh when I heard the cabin door open.

"I'm so relieved to find someone. My car broke down and I must have got turned around trying to find a shortcut to the garage. I don't know what I'd have done if you hadn't answered the door. Would it be possible for me to use your phone. Just one quick call. I promise I'm not a crazy person."

Carly!

It was Carly. How the hell had she tracked me down?

"CARLY! I'M IN THE SUGAR BOWL!"

I hollered, but I don't think my voice carried out of the bowl. I slammed my hand against the side, but all that did was help me sink further down into the sugar. I wasn't close to drowning in the stuff, but there are some places that sand and sugar just don't go. Let's just say the sugar tide was getting too close to the number one place and leave it at that.

"I don't have a phone." Jordan said after a long pause.

"Oh." Carly sounded disappointed. "Could you give me directions to the nearest mechanic?"

"No. I'm sorry I sorta just moved here. I just don't know the area that well."

"Then can I just come in and sit down for a bit? Thank you."

"I … uh … it's just … okay."

I managed to stop the sinking before the sugar reached my parts, but I had no way of getting Carly's attention or seeing what was going on outside the darkness of the bowl. I could try pounding again, but that didn't work the first time and I'd definitely get painful painful sugar up my vag.

"Wow. You really have this rustic thing down don't you?" Carly said. "Do you even have electricity? And an outhouse. Do you have an outhouse?"

"Yeah. Stella likes to live off the grid."

"Stella's your cabin mate?"

"... uh … yeah."

"Will she be back soon? Maybe she could give me directions."

"She won't be back for hours. Maybe not until after sundown."

"That's too bad." Carly said. "Are you sure there isn't anyone else I could talk to?"

"I … no."

"You don't sound so sure, Jordan."

"Did I tell you my name when I opened the door?"

"No."

"Then how did ..."

"Because a good lawyer does her research."

"Lawyer?"

"It's a scary word I know, but I'm not here to be a lawyer. I'm here to talk to you about my cousin."

"Stella?"

"No. Rebecca.."

"I don't know what you're talking about."

"Bullshit, Jordan. She's here, probably in this room, and we both know it."

"That's ... no. You're just trying to get me to talk. You don't know anything."

"I know a lot of things. I know how many beans make five. I know the law. I know how much it takes to bribe a Shrink Inc tech to have your stupid cousin, who is getting herself shrunk so she can be the sex pet of some teeny bopper, chipped."

"Chipped? Like a GPS thing?"

"Not like. It is a GPS 'thing.' And that GPS 'thing' led me three states away from home.

"I have no problem with you wanting to live the simple life out here in the woods with Stella. That's your business. I don't even care that Maria is offering a six figure reward for information of your whereabouts. Sure I have the number on speed dial, but I figure if you want to run away who am I to get in your way? I respect your choice.

"But respect is a two way street, Jordan. If I come to you asking to know where Becky is. Where a member of **my** family is. And you blow smoke up my ass. That's not being very respectful. And if you don't respect me maybe I don't respect you and Maria makes me six figures richer.

"Now tell me, Jordan. Where is Rebecca?"

"The sugar bowl."

I heard the lid move before I saw it. Loud and grating like a manhole cover getting pried up. Then I could see Carly's angelic face beaming down on me. No one. Not my mother. Not any of my ex-girlfriends. Not even Tina looked more beautiful than Carly did at that moment.

"Thank god you found me. This is what being rescued feels like."

"What are you doing in there, ya donut hole?"   Carly offered me her finger.

"It was horrible." I pulled myself to the rim of the bowl. "Jordan and me we ran into the woods and we got chased by a drone and we got separated and I was all alone in the woods overnight even though I'm smaller than a chipmunk."

I swung a leg over the bowl and slid out and onto the table. Granules of sugar flew off me when I landed on my feet.

"Do I even want to know why it's 10 in the morning and you're naked in a sugar bowl? Are those dots I even want to connect?"

"Probably not." I admitted, brushing sugar off my legs and butt.

"It's a good thing I came prepared." Carly plopped her house sized handbag down on the other side of the table and started rummaging through it.

"Look. I told you where Rebecca was. You're not going to tell Maria where I am are you?" Jordan sounded as nervous as she looked.

"That depends. I plan on walking out of your life with my cousin. Are you going to give me any trouble?"

"No." Jordan didn't sound too sure of her answer.

"Then we don't have a problem." Carly dropped a stack of clothes in front of me.

"Doll clothes?" I made a face as I sorted through the stack.

"It was that or a dress made out of a cut down Fritos bag."

"You're not really going to take her are you?" Jordan seemed dazed at the thought.

"You should come with us." I said, pulling cheap nylon doll panties over my hips.

"That didn't work out so good the last time. Anyway I'm the one who's supposed to be in charge."

"I know all that, but I also know that Stella is every bit as broken as you think she is." I said trying to navigate a bra built for plastic boobs. "You should not be here when she gets back. Trust me. I know what she's capable of when she gets pissed off."

Jordan just stood there looking like a deer who'd wandered into interstate traffic.

"I don't know exactly what's going on here, Jordan, but it sounds like maybe you should come with us." Carly said. "Assuming Little Miss Molasses Pants can get her little butt in gear."

"You could just put me in your purse and let me change in there. I've literally spent weeks getting trained in how to do that exact thing." I pulled the doll dress over my head.

"On the subject of 'literally.' I have literally no idea how many 'sugar bowls' my shrunken naked cousin has been inside today, but there's no way that letting you prance around all naked inside my purse is the hygienic option."

"Seriously, Jordan. We were just talking about this. Remember? The eyes? She may treat you nice, but you know she doesn't mean it. If she did you wouldn't be almost peeing yourself right now." I slipped my feet into the plastic shoes.

I looked her in the eyes and tried to convince her to come with us. I had a bad feeling about leaving her here for Stella to find. Like the next time I saw Jordan would be on a remake of Unsolved Mysteries.

The cabin door opened.

"If I knew you were coming I'd have stuck around a little longer." Stella said. She shut the cabin door as final as a coffin. "Who's your friend, honey?"

"... her … her car broke down." Jordan sputtered out.

"Yes." Carly said. Maybe a little too enthusiastically, but when you're in a small room with a psycho carrying a long bow who's to say how enthusiastic you should be.

"It's three miles to the nearest road." Stella advanced into the room with the bow in her hands. She almost made it look like she was holding it casually, but I could see her knuckles strain.

"Yeah, I tried to find a short cut through the forest. I must have wandered twice that distance before I lucked out and found your cabin. You don't know how thankful I am to find this place. My name's Carly by the way."

Carly was backing away as Stella walked towards her.

"How long ago did it happen?" Stella asked. She was past the table backing Carly into a corner. Her hand wasn't on the bowstring, but I was guessing it wouldn't take her long to get it there.

"What?" Carly's back brushed against the log wall.

"Your flat tire." Stella was almost touching her.

"Stella please." Jordan's voice was smaller than me.

"I don't have a flat tire. My car just broke down. … I think it was maybe the battery."

"The battery?" Stella's face was inches from Carly's

"Maybe. I'm no expert."

Stella stood there deep inside Carly's personal space and just stared at the manically smiling attorney.

"You're lucky you found us then." Stella took a step back and smiled. Jordan and I let out the breath we didn't realize we had been holding.

"About when did your battery … or whatever quit on you?" Stella asked.

"A couple hours ago. Give or take. I'm a bit turned around right now."

"I bet."

"Yeah with all that walking and getting lost."

"The thing is this, Carly. You don't mind if I call you that, do you?"

"No."

"The thing is, Carly I've seen you before."

"I've got one of those faces."

"I've seen you spying on us. The past two nights. On the other side of the north tree line."

"No. That's just crazy … No."

"I bet you thought you were being all sneaky, but these are my woods, bitch and no one comes to my home and makes a fool of me." I didn't see Stella draw the arrow, but it was wedged up to the bowstring by the time she finished talking. She was aiming for Carly's face. "Now tell me why you're here, why I shouldn't kill you, and why I should believe a liar."

Jordan cried something I couldn't understand. Carly just stared at the arrow too scared to speak. I didn't know what to say until a really stupid idea popped in my head.

"Jordan. There's something I have to tell you." I yelled at my owner until she looked my way. "It's about Stella and what she did to me in the woodshed. What she told me not to tell you."

"Shut the fuck up, Dumbelina." Stella said in a monotone voice scarier than a scream.

"She made me dance for her. Sort of a stripper ballet thing. There was a costume and everything. She fapped off while I did my little ballet stripper routine.

"She's lying, honey." Stella was speaking to Jordan, but her eyes were still on Carly.

"Then when she was finished she used a buck knife to peel me out of the fetish outfit she'd dressed me in. Said that if I told you. If I made her look bad in front of you. That she'd skin me instead of the tutu."

"Stella?" Jordan looked scared. Scared that she was right about her new lover.

I needed to get Stella to turn away from Carly. Get so mad at me that she did something stupid and give Carly a chance to run. In my defense it was only as stupid as most of my other plans.

"That's not all." I said. "You know those marks on my butt? The ones I told you were from falling off you in the woods? I was lying. She made me lie to you or she was going to take me back to the woodshed to get threatened and drooled over."

"What'd she do?" Jordan asked.

"She branded me."

"Like cattle?"

"Don't listen to her. This is another one of her trick escape attempts."

"Exactly like cattle." I said. "If you don't believe me come over here and get a good close look."

I turned myself around and did the best William Wallace I could in a doll dress and panties. I was turned away so I couldn't see, but I could hear Jordan's giant body quake its way over to where I mooned.

"shit" I could feel Jordan's exhale better than I could hear the word she said making it.

I didn't feel Stella shake the world the same way Jordan had. Stella was a hunter and this was her home so I shouldn't have been too surprised that she could move like that that quietly, but I was. One minute I was bent over at the waist pointing my butt up to the Jordan sky, the next I was knocked down onto my side trying not to trip on the skirt of the cheap dress as I scrambled backwards away from Stella.

I didn't know where Jordan was. I hoped she and Carly were running out the door, but I didn't hear their giant footsteps. Stella was looking down at me fumbling around on the table. She'd dropped the bow and replaced it with the same buck knife she'd used to humiliate me in the woodshed.

Her hands moved with the impossible speed giants had, only faster. I felt the ground explode under me and when I could see the knife again it was buried half my height into the wooden table. I tried to move away, but couldn't. A terrified part of me thought that Stella had pinned me to the table like a butterfly, but then I realized she had only pinned the skirt of my dress.

Stella said something, but I was too freaked out to tell you what it was she said. She pulled the knife out of the wood. I could feel the table lift off the ground when she did. The knife had been in there hard and deep. It didn't want to come out. Stella said something else. Maybe it was "goodbye," but I don't know. Then she brought the knife down again. I don't know how I knew, but I knew this time she was aiming for my heart.

A lifetime of bad movies and good TV taught me that when the shit hits the fan everything goes slo mo. It happened to me when the giant knife came barreling down at my tiny heart. I could see every subtle expression play over Stella's billboard sized face. Could see the light glistening off the blade. Watch as it came down closer and closer to me.

I caught a splash of red out of the top of my eye, but I couldn't take my eyes away from the knife long enough to figure out what it was. That was when Stella screamed. Not some BS "we slowed the film down" crap, a real scream in real time.

I forced my eyes closed when the knife was still a few inches above me. I hoped it wouldn't hurt and that it'd be over quick. I didn't really believe in god and didn't pick then to start so there was no use praying.

I felt the ground under me shudder just like it had before. I could hear the sharp metal being pushed through the wood. My little body was thrown almost an inch up in the air from the force.

It didn't feel like I'd been stabbed. And if I'd been pinned I couldn't have been tossed in the air, could I? Unless she'd cut me in two and I was in shock and feeling ghost sensations from my severed bottom half. I wondered if my other half imagined it was whole too.

I turned my head to the left and opened my eyes. I didn't want the first part of the last thing I ever saw to be my dangling guts. I saw my reflection in the shiny metal of the blade embedded in the table three inches from my head. My reflection and I both looked as freaked out as I felt, but we were still breathing.

A splash of red fell down from up above and landed on my chest. Technically it was a drop, but at my size it hit me like a liquid fist and exploded in a copper smelling splatter that covered me from my face to my knees.

Blood.

I looked up in time to see Stella push Carly away. There was something buried in Stella's neck and blood on Carly's hands. It was an arrow. Carly had stabbed Stella with her own effing arrow. Carly had just saved my life.

Have I told you how much I love my cousin?

A giant hand plucked me off the table. It took me a second to tell who had grabbed me, but I saw Stella trying to stop the bleeding with a t-shirt and Jordan getting dragged along by the hand not holding me.

That left my favorite cousin.

"I have a SUV parked near here." Carly said after she'd passed the cabin door and was out of Stella's earshot. "GPS will get us out of here and we can send the police after Stella."

"You bought a SUV just to rescue me?"

"It's a rental. Now shut up and let me rescue you."

We were all in shock. At least a little bit. Jordan worst of all. After the woman with an arrow in her neck, but she was a dick to me so I wasn't counting her. Jordan didn't fight, but she was so limp she was dragging us down. I kept looking back at the cabin thinking that I'd see Stella run out ala Jason, ready to shoot us down.

Yeah, I know Jason used a machete, not a long bow. I'm going for that psycho in the woods vibe.

We'd put a lot of ground between us and the cabin, but I wished we could go faster. But neither one of my giants was the jogging kind of gal so I had to make due with a lawyer's pace. It was still super faster than anything I could have pulled off with my little legs so I probably shouldn't complain.

We went over a small hill and came down into a ravine that came equipped with an escape vehicle. It looked like a rental, but it also looked beautiful. Carly pushed Jordan into the backseat, dropped me in the driver's cup holder, and got behind the wheel. The keys were already in it. Just one turn and we were out of there.

Nothing.

Carly tried turning the key again and got more of the same.

"Comeoncomeoncomeon." Carly begged the car to start, but it was a heartless bastard.

"I think Stella cut the fuel line." Jordan said from the back. It was the only thing she's said since we'd left the cabin.

"That's a really weird thing to say there, Jordan."

"Did Stella tell you she cut the fuel line?" Carly asked. She was pissed. "Did you know we were running to a useless pile of crap."

"No. No. I just sm..."

Whatever it was Jordan was about to say got drowned out by what happened next. I think I may have heard a rifle fire.

I definitely heard the explosion.

Eleven: The Stapler's Cousin

I didn't dream.

At least I don't think so. Or maybe I did and I can't remember it. I do remember waking up in short bursts then falling right back unconscious. Like I wasn't a person anymore, just a computer that was having trouble getting restarted. Coming on and turning right off cause something was really wrong somewhere in my computer guts.

I did that a lot, I think. Then one time I woke up and it stuck.

"I'm awake now. Any second now I'm going to open my eyes and everything is just going to be hunky dory. There isn't going to be anything weird. I'm not going to be trapped in my own giant undies. I'm not going to be dressed up in some weird fetish gear. No one's going to try to hurt me, or scare me, or make me into their domme. It's just gonna be nice and normal. Relatively."

I managed to say that all with my outer voice. I found out later I was still coming down from some pretty serious pain killers so I'll use that as an excuse if I sounded loopy back there.

I opened my eyes and saw a ceiling directly above me. I was laying down on what felt like a bed facing up. I just stared at the drop ceiling for several seconds trying to put my finger on what was wrong with this picture. Then it clicked – the ceiling was normal ceiling height above me. I could stand on the bed and touch it if I wanted to.

And I did.

I looked down from the height of the bed I was standing on and took in the room. It looked like a pretty standard hospital room sized for a pretty standard lady. There were a couple small banks of monitors going "beep" beside me. There were cords connecting them to various patches on my arms and neck. I could feel a draft on my back and I realized I was in a johnny and it wasn't tied up properly.

"It's good to see you up, Ms. Hogarth, but maybe it's a little early for you to be that 'up.'"

It was a man's voice coming from right behind me.

I yanked the loose ends of the johnny together and spun around. The machines made a serious of angry beeps, but I wasn't worried about them so much as what this stranger had gotten to see.

"Did you see my butt?" I know it was a stupid question, but I think I was owed a few of them after all I'd been through.

"Yes, Ms. Hogarth." The man in the nice suit said. He was my size. Probably. At least he was close enough that I looked down on him while standing on the bed.

"OK. Glad we got that settled." I said, carefully pulling the johnny tight around me and stepping down from the bed. "I think I'm supposed to ask where I am. Cause I don't know and you look like you do."

"You're in my home, Ms. Hogarth." He said. He offered me his hand to shake.

"This looks like a hospital room." I used one hand to keep my butt covered and used the other to shake his hand. I stretched my arm out as far as it would go keeping the rest of me as far from him as I could without being completely rude. "You have a hospital room in your home?"

"It comes in handy from time to time."

"How long have I been here? And what happened to Carly and Jordan? And Stella? She didn't get away did she? I'm gonna punch something if she got away."

"Ms. Vintner and Ms. Brewster are recovering. Stella is recovering in police custody. You've been here 33 days."

"33 DAYS!"

"You had third degree burns over 90 percent of your body, but now you look like the worst thing that happened to that lovely skin of yours was a mild sunburn. My science can create miracles, Ms. Hogarth, but even it takes time."

"'Your science?'" I asked. It was that or think about the creepy skin comment.

"I'm Richard Stovent."

"As in The Stovent Corporation? Shrink Inc?"

"I hate that nickname, but yes."

"OK. OK." The words were tumbling out of my mouth. "This is going to sound wicked crazy, but this room looks pretty normal. And it doesn't hurt my neck to look you in the eye. But I remember being shrunk. Real tiny. Not as small as Walter, but smaller than Lisa. Was that me just pulling a Patrick Duffy? Was that a dream? Or did you cure me? You cured me. This is great. I can go back to being me."

"Gretchen!" He called out.

"Huh?"

He smiled like a snake and pointed to the wall behind me. I put both hands on the back of the johnny just in case this was a trick to see my butt again and turned to look. He was pointing at a window. I don't remember what I'd seen out it before, but it wasn't a giant eye framed by a huge, yet delicate, eyebrow.

The eye stared straight into me then winked.

"Oh." I said, deflated.

"Exactly."

"So you're ..."

"Yes."

"And Gretchen's your ..."

"Employee."

"I was going to say owner, but OK." I said. "Was there an accident? Did you piss off the necromancers? Did they do this to you cause you shorted their 401K?"

"It wasn't anything I wanted, Ms. Hogarth. Perhaps one day I'll tell you the story, but not today."

"Wow. OK. I noticed you didn't deny necromancer involvement. Mental note taken. But what do you want with me?"

"This wasn't how I planned on meeting you, Ms. Hogarth. Originally I was going to have a word in private with you before you were due to be sold to Tina Jordan, but mistakes were made. If I understand the circumstances correctly you then made mistakes of your own that only made the situation infinitely more complicated."

"So you're going to fix things?" I had a bad feeling about this.

"Possibly."

"Can you vague that up for me?"

"It all depends on what you would consider 'fixed,' Ms. Hogarth. You're in a most precarious position. I could just let things run their course for good or ill or I could directly intervene."

"Huh?"

"I may be resized, Ms. Hogarth, but I am still a very powerful man. It may not be a power that I can wield legally or under the full scrutiny of the world, but the same can be said for dozens of other great men and women in our history. People who molded the course of history from behind the scenes.

"Let me ask you this question, Ms. Hogarth. Do you regret your decision to be shrunk?"

"Every day."

"I thought so. The vast majority of our subjects have the desire to be like we are now. It's their dream. Fantasy. Fetish. But not yours or mine. We want nothing more than to live our lives in as close an approximation to normal as every other human being on the face of this world. My money and power have allowed me to do so. I could make that happen for you as well."

"What's the catch?" There was always a catch.

"That you stay with me. Become my companion."

"'Companion' like being your best bud you hang out with watching Sherlock reruns? Or the kind that fuck?."

"Both. Given time."

"You want me to be your girlfriend?"

"Insofar as any marriage between us wouldn't be legal. Yes."

"And if I say no?"

"Things will play out the way they would have." He said. "You'll have to deal with your owner, her former employer, the woman who paid to have you shrunk, and the legal team of my company trying to absolve me of any blame in the whole matter."

"Is that all?" I asked.

"Isn't it enough?"

"Yeah it's … huge. But I was more concerned about me getting bumped off for knowing your big secret. Isn't that what men like you do to women like me?"

"You aren't the first woman I've approached with this offer, Ms. Hogarth. They are all alive. As far as I know."

"So you're gonna wipe my memory or something?"

"I'm going to rely on you to not tell anyone."

"You've known me five minutes, do you think I know how to keep my mouth shut?"

"Most people will assume that you are either insane or a publicity whore. But if you do manage to convince someone in the media or the authorities that I am what I am then Gretchen will pay you a visit."

"Gretchen?"

"No matter where you are."

"What's Gretchen gonna do?"

"I really have no idea, Ms. Hogarth. It's best that way. But whatever she does it is 100% effective."

"Oh."

"I need an answer. Will you be my intimate companion or will you take your chances with the situation you're in? It's the lady or the tiger time, Ms. Hogarth."

I took a seat on the bed.

"You do know I'm gay, right?"

"Nobody's perfect."

"Can't you just do me this one little favor and we'll just be friends? I mean you just laid down that sweet Billy Wilder reference. We could be pals. Pals who don't touch genitals."

"I'm not asking for that kind of companionship."

"No. Of course you're not. You're just asking me to be swept away by a handsome, young-ish, billionaire with a company that makes magic technology. You're offering me the chance to live the illusion of a normal life; all I gotta do is spread my legs for you every once in a while and give you an after dinner blowie on your b-day. If I were straight I'd be wet right now. But I'm not. I hope you find someone else. I really do. Being this small sucks on toast. It's lonely and isolating and even worse because you didn't want to be this way.

"I'm sorry, but I can't take you up on your offer, Richard."

He stood there for a minute not speaking while I sat on the bed waiting for him to make the next move.

"Too bad." He finally said. "I rather liked your butt."

"That took forever." Lauren poked through the last of the take out boxes. "You need to brevity it up next time. And order more food. I can't believe we ran out of noodles."

If this had been an old tyme movie it would have been cutting back and forth from a clock on the wall and me standing there in my little witness box getting tireder and tireder as I went on. There'd be music stings and weird angles when they cut between the clock and me.

Only there was no witness box, only the hamster cage that I'd been put back into. Also it was nowadays not 1947 and nowadays when people needed to know the time they just look at their phones. I wasn't people anymore so no phone and no idea how many hours I'd been babbling. I talked through at least one lunch, five potty breaks (there's some wood shavings in the corner that need to be changed), and a lot of dazed expressions. Somewhere in all of that Carly shared some of her pad thai. I tried to avoid drinking from the hamster bottle, but after all that time talking my throat overruled my pride and I lapped away.

The doll clothes had drip dried to my body hours ago. They were annoying and scratchy before, now they were stiff, annoying, and even scratchier. Every part of me that was touching cloth felt like ants were crawling all over me.

At least I hadn't pulled the doll panties back up. The last thing I needed right now was crunchy underpants.

Everyone looked as exhausted and hungry as I felt. The two hungriest were looking straight at me.

"All of that really happened?" Maria asked. There was something different about her face. It was still hard as rock, but at that moment it looked like it just might soften.

"Cross my heart." And I did.

OK, so I skipped the part about Richard Stovent waking me up to make a pretty decent indecent proposal. The truth drug must have been wearing off and it seemed like the sort of thing best to just shut up about.

"That one." Maria pointed to Lauren. "Did those things to you?"

"And more."

"And you really did try to track down Jordan after you fell?"

"I'm super small and I totally flunked outdoors as a kid, but, yeah. I tried."

"Irrelevant." McCaskill said. "The letter of the law dictates that this pet was supposed to be offered for sale to my client."

"She kidnapped my friend, you heartless bitch. Don't we deserve justice?"

"Ms. Alvarez, this pet is no more culpable for her actions than that stapler is. She may look and sound like a person, but she isn't. If you were gullible enough to allow this stapler to trick you than you and your 'friend' got what you deserve."

I felt my body respond to McCaskill's demeaning words. I didn't think I was a sub, but when that woman talked down to me my insides went fifty shades of McCaskill.

"I spent six figures on that stapler and you can bet she's coming home with us."

"Does the stapler get a vote?" I asked.

"No." Maria and McCaskill unisoned me.

"Actually she might."

The two women fighting over me looked over at Claire.

"In all versions of events it is clear that an agent of our company made a mistake. One that she has paid for dearly."

"You didn't shrink her did you?" I asked. "You didn't shrink her and put her in her own pet shop? Lisa's probably already made her her bitch. Maybe even Lola too.”

“Had that employee not made the mistake she did then Becky would have been given her legal right to refuse or accept her sale to Ms. Jordan.” Claire just kept on talking like I hadn't said anything. But she didn't deny it either. So it totally happened that way.

“I don't think I like where this is leading, Claire.” Maria said.

“I'm assuming that your client wants to complete the sale, Ms. McCaskill.” Claire stated.

“She does.”

“Then all Becky has to do is agree to the sale and we can look into finding a replacement tiny for Ms. Alvarez and Jordan. Otherwise she becomes the property of Stovent to be disposed of any way we see fit.”

“Let me guess, that way's going to be Maria.” I said.

“I'm not authorized to tell you that, but it's certainly an option.” Claire said. “Going to the Pet Shop for real is another. But right now all you have to worry your pretty little head about is whether you accept Tina's offer.”

“I don't know.” I sat down on a bare part of the cage and put my head in my hands. My little heart was jackhammering inside my chest. “I've been drugged. I'm worn out. Hungry. And my dress is crunchy. Can't we just circle around and get back to this tomorrow?”

“That's not an option.” McCaskill said.

“It should be.” I shot back. I didn't bother looking up at her.

“Don't you love Tina?”

It was the first thing I'd heard Jordan say all day. I lifted my head from my knees and looked straight into her staring blue eyes. They looked so adorable framed by her giant bangs.

“No.”

The room went silent as that sunk in.

“I thought I did. I really really did. She's so … perfect. And I'm so not. I've been talking about my life forever and every time I said I loved Tina it got weird. Like I loved her in the past when I was saying and feeling all those things. And now I don't. Maybe it's the drugs talking. Maybe I just tricked myself into thinking I loved her cause I wanted it so bad.”

“Irrelevant.” McCaskill said. “My client wants you, she has paid for you, and she's willing to give you a much better life than you deserve.”

“That's all true. Maybe the smart thing to do is say yes to the purse and become Tina's 'plus one/tenth' on the red carpet, but she doesn't love me. This is one of the most important scariest days of my life and she can't even call me."

"If you don't love Tina … do you … do you love me?" Jordan looked like her life depended on my answer.

"No. Not like that."

Her face fell and my heart broke.

"Love or no love, we still need your decision, Becky." Claire rubbed the spot between the corners of her eyes and the sides of her nose. "Or one will be made for you."

I put my head back in my hands. I wanted to be a hawk flying through the sky or a mermaid splashing around in the sea with the other merladies. I wanted to be anything or anywhere, but Becky Hogarth sitting on this table on this day making this decision.

I wasn't looking, but I could tell that the light filtering through the bars of the hamster cage had stopped. I felt the ground beneath my crunchy butt shift as a great weight came down somewhere nearby. I'd been a tiny long enough to know it meant one of the giants was looming over me. Probably McCaskill trying to intimidate me into saying yes.

"Look at me, Rebecca."

Carly's face was right in front of me when I looked up. Her face took up almost the entire side of the cage I was looking out.

"There are a lot of people telling you what you 'have' to do right now. What do you want to do?"

"I want to be big again."

"That's not possible."

"Then I want to go home with you. You're the only one here who loves me. You're the only one who's there for me."

"That's not on the table, Becky." Claire said. "There are two people with competing claims for you and even if there weren't there's no way your cousin could afford to pay for you. And it's not like we're just going to give you to her."

"But what if you did?" Carly turned from me to face Claire. "What if everyone got what they want?"

"Jesus Fucking Christ!" McCaskill tossed her pen across the room and turned to Claire. "End this. One way or the other so I can either bring Tina her new toy or file a suit that's going to bring this place to the ground."

Claire stared down McCaskill for several seconds before finally speaking. "What do I want, Ms Vintner?" Claire didn't take her eyes off McCaskill.

"That's easy. You want this to be done with the least amount of trouble."

"It seems to me that the easiest way to do that is to give Becky to one of these ladies." Claire said.

"McCaskill already said what we've all been thinking." Carly started walking around the room. "If she loses here she's going to wage legal war on your ass, Claire. And just because Maria doesn't have representation here doesn't mean she won't lawyer up. And you know how the press just loves talking about that weird company that shrinks perverts and sells them to other pervs."

"HEY!" I squeaked from inside my cage.

"I didn't mean you. Just hush and let me try to save your butt."

"OK, H&R Blockhead, I'll play along." McCaskill wasn't holding back. "What do I want?"

"A win."

"A win?"

"A nice big juicy one you can dangle in front of Tina Jordan when you plop all those billable hours on her desk. One so big she's just gonna have her people sign the check without batting an eye."

Carly had walked around to McCaskill's side of the table.

"What do you want?" Carly pointed directly at Maria. I thought it was rude, but Carly was a lawyer so she maybe knew what she was doing.

"Revenge." Replied the maid turned mistress.

"Boring."

"You asked." Maria shrugged with just her face.

"I'm not saying 'no' right now, but maybe there's something else."

"I just … I just want Jordan to be happy."

"Got it." Carly's pointing finger moved to Jordan. "And what does Jordan want?"

"I want to be owned. By Maria. Really owned, not this fake slavery thing we have going."

"You know that's not possible." Maria's voice was so much softer when talking to Jordan. "The law won't let us."

"Not if I'm resized."

"OK. Didn't see that one coming." I said from my place on the floor of my cage.

"We've been over this, Jordan." Maria sounded like she was explaining to a three year old why she couldn't have cotton candy for supper. "I'm not gay. Or a domme. I can't give you what you really want. Not directly."

"I'm straight too." Carly said. "This isn't about sex, this is about helping the people you love. And you love Jordan as much as I love Becky."

"I love you too, Carly."

"Alright so let's go down our list." Carly started ticking down on her fingers. "McCaskill wants a win. Becky wants me. I want Becky. Jordan wants to belong to Maria. Maria wants Jordan to be happy …"

"And revenge." Maria reminded us.

" … and maybe revenge, and Claire just wants this to go away."

"Aren't you going to ask me what I want?" Lauren asked.

"You're the intern, Lauren." I said. "Nobody cares what you want."

"Yeah, but I have five times more reason to be here than Carly."

"What do you want, Lauren?" Carly asked. She was about as unhappy about it as I was.

"More time with Becky."

"Not on the table." I said, standing up.

"What?" Carly asked. I didn't know why, this wasn't going to happen.

"Not cause I love her or I'm gay or any other stupid shit like that. You see her as a victim, I see her as my lab rat. And I still haven't finished researching her."

"How long would you need?" Carly asked.

"No time." I called up. I couldn't believe Carly even asked the question. "Remember 'not on the table.'"

"A month would be perfect, but I'd settle for two weeks."

I was about to tell her she'd settle for none, but not even Carly was listening to me. No one listens to you when you're three and a half inches.

Carly's walk turned into a pace as she processed all of this. Claire and McCaskill checked their phones. Maria checked Jordan.

"This is so exciting." Jordan said. "It's like we walked into the last chapter of an Agatha Christie story where the detective tells everyone whodunnit."

"Except the stakes are **much** higher." I said.

"You're the stakes, short round." Lauren snarked. "The only way you're getting any higher is if someone tosses you out a window."

"Shut up, Lauren."

"I've got it." Carly finally said.

"This I have got to hear." McCaskill said.

"I may not be the kind of lawyer you are, Ms. McCaskill. I may not have the kind of clients you have. I may only be the stapler's cousin. But I am every bit as smart and determined as you are. Now sit still and keep your pie hole shut while I make my pitch, bitch."

Maybe it was a good thing Carly wasn't a trial lawyer. McCaskill didn't look happy, but she didn't storm out either.

"To start with, Becky is going to turn down Tina's offer."

"I am?"

"But not just yet. This is just the dress rehearsal to make sure we all have the same script."

"That may satisfy the law, strip mall lawyer, but not my client." McCaskill said. "We'll sue."

"Not if Stovent gives you something even better than Becky." Carly countered.

"Such as …"

"Paige."

"The tiny ethnologist in the Pet Shop? Why would my client be interested in that?"

"What's better than buying a human purse pet? Adopting a rescue tiny."

"I'm listening, Ms. Vintner."

"Everybody knows that before there were human pets Stovent shrank down normally huge animals to be house pets. Everyone's seen the iconic shot of Glenda Merronwie with her Oscar in one hand and an adult elephant in the other."

"I remember the stink from the SPCA and PETA over that." Maria said. "There were ads against it everywhere."

"Then Ophelia Cornish adopted the first human purse pet and everyone agreed that it was better to have someone who signed up for the job rather than some dumb animal unlucky enough to get caught and shrank.

"Now dozens of celebrities have their own human pets. The novelty is starting to wear off. But if Tina were to adopt a woman like Paige. With her story. With her background. Tina could reinvent herself as a Tiny Rights Activist. Her owning Paige could be used to show just how superior Tina is to all those shallow A-listers who treat their shrunken people as trophies. Hell, she could throw a few thousand dollars at Paige's research to make it look good."

"And we'd give Becky and Paige away out of the goodness of our hearts?" Claire said. "I'm also a little leery about this whole Tiny Rights idea. Sounds like something that would just blow up in our face."

"Becky and Paige are part of the cost of making this go away." Carly said. "It's cheaper and less embarrassing than a series of very public trials.

"As for any Tiny Rights blowback. They're celebrities. Nobody takes them seriously. The only thing that's going to happen is a lot more people are going to be talking about your company. And a lot of celebrities are going to be following Tina's lead and rescuing 'victims" of your pet shop. Think of Becky and Paige as loss leaders."

"Wait." I said. "Tina doesn't want me for publicity. The whole idea was that she'd have tiny me to lesperiment on. Maybe my gaydar didn't shrink with me, but I'm pretty sure Paige is straight."

"So's spaghetti until you get it hot and wet." It was the first time I'd seen McCaskill truly smile.

"Paige won't have to get … whatever." Carly said waving away the mental imagery. "Paige is going to need to interview tinies as part of her research. I can only imagine the years of interview required to get a fair picture of Jordan."

"Jordan's not a tiny." Maria stated.

"But she wants to be." Carly said. "The only objection you had to that was that you weren't able to be her domme lover. Well Tina wants a tiny girlfriend on the side and McCaskill seems like the kind of lady who knows her way around a dungeon. Paige can be a beard. More or less."

"And Stovent would use the money I spent on Becky to shrink Jordan?"

"You'd be getting a significant price break if we did." Claire said. "Of course we'd expect no litigation coming your way. If we did."

"And Lauren could use Jordan as her new test subject." Carly tried to sneak that one through, but Maria wasn't having any of that.

"No. I'm not sure if I'm cool leaving Jordan with her," Maria gestured at McCaskill, "there's no way I'm leaving her alone with her."

"You can give Lauren guidelines. Tell her what she can and can't do." Carly was still trying to sell it, but I could tell from Maria's face she wasn't picking up what Carly was laying down.

"That's true, Ms. Alvarez, but didn't you say you wanted revenge?" Claire asked. "Becky clearly hates Lauren. Wouldn't it be a fitting punishment to make Becky spend the next month under Lauren's thumb?"

"Or in her pants?" McCaskill chimed in.

"NO!" I was rattling the bars on my tiny cage.

"There's no way I'm letting that woman get her hands back on my cousin. Did you hear what she did to her already? I don't even want to think about what she has planned next."

"Lauren can be given guidelines." Maria said. "You can tell her what she can and can't do."

"She's using your words against you, Carly." I said. "Make her stop."

"Correction." McCaskill said. "I can give her trainer guidelines."

"What?"

"Legally the training portion of the contract takes place before the final sale." McCaskill explained. "Since my client was the one who paid for the resizing she is the one who has the right to dictate terms of training. My client has delegated that power to me."

Fuckityfuckfuck

"You have got to be kidding me?" I couldn't read Carly's expression I was too busy freaking out.

"That would be my interpretation as well." Claire said.

"I'm willing to go along with Ms. Vintner's plan if Stovent and Maria are." McCaskill said. "So long as Lauren follows my training guidelines and Maria gets her revenge."

Maria nodded.

"My company will be good with this." Claire said. "What about you, Ms. Vintner?"

"Becky?" Carly looked down at where I was freaking out in my cage.

"So Lauren the dick is going to have complete control of my life for the next month and the only thing keeping her from totally fucking me over is McCaskill's ethics?"

"I can promise you you're property will be alive and physically intact when she is delivered to you, Vintner." McCaskill said. "I don't need to leave marks to cause pain."

"I tried, honey. I really did." Carly leaned down close and whispered over me. "But this is the best I could do. You could just say yes and become Tina's purse pet. She doesn't love you, but she isn't going to put you through whatever that bitch Lauren has up her sleeve."

"But I want to be with you."

Carly lowered a giant finger into the cage and rubbed it against my cheek.

"I know. But the only way for you to be with me is to go through a month of Hell. I'm not worth that."

"You are. Did you hear how many times I said I wish I'd just listened to you? A gazillion. You tracked me down. A psycho with a gun blew you up cause of me. And you still want to help me. You are totally worth a month of Lauren Hell."

"I don't even know how I'll take care of you. I don't make that much. Do I need to find someone to watch you while I'm at work? Can I take you to work? How are things going to work between us?"

"We can worry about that after Lauren."

"Are you sure about this?"

"I'd rather be with family who love me than some super hot sex goddess."

"Sounds like someone's grown up."

"Don't after school special the moment, you dork." I rubbed my face on her finger and gave it a gentle kiss. "This is what I want."

"I hope you're right, sweetie. I hope you're right."

9 798389 852402